for ... e book
... Thomas.

110652402

Praise for the Erskine Powell series

MALICE IN THE HIGHLANDS

"A story that carries you along, set in beautiful country—vividly and realistically brought to life. You read it—and are there!"
—ANNE PERRY

"*Malice in the Highlands* is the perfect choice for readers nostalgic for the good old-fashioned British village mystery."
—*Alfred Hitchcock Mystery Magazine*

MALICE IN CORNWALL

"The Cornish mists and sea swirl constantly in the background of *Malice in Cornwall*, a murder mystery that can also be read as a travel book.... Graham Thomas certainly knows how to exploit the air of romance, mystery, and danger that still hovers over Cornwall."
—SUSAN ALLEN TOTH,
Author of *England for All Seasons*

"Readers will find the unraveling of this fascinating mystery and the continued untangling of Powell's character equally impressive."
—*Publishers Weekly*

By Graham Thomas
Published by Ivy Books:

MALICE IN THE HIGHLANDS
MALICE IN CORNWALL
MALICE ON THE MOORS

MALICE ON THE MOORS

Graham Thomas

IVY BOOKS • NEW YORK

An Ivy Book
Published by The Ballantine Publishing Group
Copyright © 1999 by Gordon Kosakoski

All rights reserved under International and Pan-American Copyright Conventions. Published in the United States by The Ballantine Publishing Group, a division of Random House, Inc., New York, and simultaneously in Canada by Random House of Canada Limited, Toronto.

Ivy Books and colophon are trademarks of Random House, Inc.

www.randomhouse.com/BB/

Library of Congress Catalog Card Number: 99-94294

ISBN 0-8041-1839-6

Manufactured in the United States of America

First Edition: August 1999

10   9   8   7   6   5   4   3   2   1

ACKNOWLEDGMENTS

The valley of Brackendale is a figment of my imagination, impossibly situated between the actual valleys of Farndale and Rosedale in the North York Moors National Park. To those who know the North York Moors, I apologize for taking geographical liberties.

I wish to thank the following individuals for their generous assistance: Superintendent Nick O'Brien of the Metropolitan Police Service; Matthew Elliot of the U.K. Pesticide Safety Directorate; John Haigh of the Countryside Alliance; Dr. Darryl McNaughton, Head of Pathology, and Graham Boffey, toxicologist (retired), Royal Inland Hospital, Kamloops, B.C.; Sue Rees, Ecologist with the North York Moors National Park Authority; Gary Overend, Campaign for Real Ale, Huddersfield and District Branch; Tony Riby, proprietor of the King's Head Hotel in Kirkbymoorside; and Peter N. Walker. Any errors, of course, are mine.

Lastly, I'd like to thank Joe Blades, my editor, for his patience, support, and unflagging enthusiasm.

As the flood begins,
Out of the fountainhead
Of fear, rage red, manalive,
Molten and mountainous to stream
Over the wound asleep
Sheep white hollow farms

—DYLAN THOMAS
Author's Prologue, *Collected Poems 1934–1952*

PROLOGUE

Harry Settle, head keeper of the Blackamoor shoot in North Yorkshire, could not dispel a nagging sense of unease as he looked out over the sea of purple heather. He was always a bit edgy on the Glorious Twelfth, the first day of the shooting season, being naturally concerned, as any field commander would be, that operations should run smoothly. And a grouse shoot is, for all intents and purposes, a highly organized military campaign. The small army of beaters were his infantry, the line of guns concealed in their stone shooting butts his artillery. This year, however, he had something else to worry about.

There had been rumors of a protest by a group of anti–blood sport fanatics, supposedly concerned about cruelty to animals or some such rubbish but dedicated in reality to destroying a way of life they knew nothing about. At least that's the way the old gamekeeper saw it. Last year a gang of them had terrorized a party of Americans on Ilkley Moor and had threatened to strike again this season. He had taken precautions, of course, but young Mr. Dinsdale had made it clear that he would hold him *personally* responsible should there be any trouble. So far, however, the shoot had gone off without a hitch, with a tally of twenty-six brace of grouse for the three morning drives. A respectable bag for a small shoot like Blackamoor, Settle reckoned with a feeling of pride. And at seventy-five quid a brace from his paying guests, Mr. Dinsdale should be pleased.

His employer had been in typical form at lunch, drinking more wine than he could hold and regaling his guests with off-color stories. It always made Settle cringe with embarrassment. However—in keeping with the occasion—it was a glorious summer day, and as he'd sat outside the shooting cabin, eating his sandwiches with the rest of the help, he'd overheard several complimentary remarks from the guests inside about his wife's veal-and-ham pie. It was the part of the day he enjoyed the most: chatting with his colleagues about which gun shot well or otherwise, the hen harrier someone saw during the drive, livestock prices, or some local scandal. And there was never a shortage of scandal, it seemed, when it came to Miss Felicity Jamieson, young Mr. Dinsdale's attractive stepsister. Settle had long ago abandoned his halfhearted attempts—made largely out of a sense of loyalty to old Mr. Dinsdale—to defend her honor. Today at lunch, the latest gossip about Miss Jamieson's exploits with a young farmer from Rosedale had been particularly vivid, to the point where even his underkeeper, Mick Curtis, had looked uncomfortable.

After the guests had finished their port and smoked their cigars, Settle had driven the guns in the Land Rover to another part of the moor for the afternoon's shooting, while his assistant transported the beaters by truck to the starting point of the drive. And now, as his eyes searched the familiar landscape for anything out of place, Settle experienced a thrill of anticipation as he always did just before the start of a drive, a feeling that had not diminished after more than forty years as a game-keeper. He saw that the beaters were in position—ten men, fifty yards apart, visible on the skyline nearly half a mile away. He frowned. He had hoped to recruit a few more lads from the local farms, but he had trouble enough finding anyone that would come to work for the paltry few pounds that Mr. Dinsdale offered. Without the promise of unlimited free beer at the end of the day, he doubted he would have got more than half a dozen volunteers this year. How different it had been in the old days, when shooting was a way of life in the dale and keepering a respected profession. Scores of keepers had once been employed in the North York Moors; now there was just a handful like himself to carry on the tradi-tion, members of a dying breed.

His assistant, Mick, was a case in point. The lad some-times seemed more concerned with the size of his tips than doing a good job. And even more worrisome, he seemed to get on particularly well with young Mr. Dins-dale, to the point where Settle sometimes felt the need to look over his shoulder.

He turned to see if the guns were ready. As usual, Mr. Dinsdale had his head up above the cut-heather blocks that were set atop the low stone walls of his shooting butt. He was swinging the muzzle of his shotgun from side to side in an unsafe manner, muttering something to himself. Or maybe, Settle thought, he's talking to his father. He could picture old Mr. Dinsdale slumped in his wheelchair at the back of the butt, staring vacantly into space. They wheeled him out every August for the opening shoot and then wheeled him back to the big house, not to be seen again for another year. The keeper shook his head. It was sad really. The old squire used to love his shooting, and despite being "new" money, he had been a generous and gracious master. Not like his bloody offspring—Settle had to make an effort to restrain himself. After all, there was no point in complaining; he wasn't getting any younger, and he had a wife and his future security to worry about.

The flankers, three to a side, stood in a line thirty yards apart on either end and forward of the line of butts, white flags at the ready. As the drive progressed they would move away from the butts towards the ends of the advancing line of beaters, thus containing the grouse in a trapezoidal enclosure, the line of beaters and the row of butts representing the long and short sides, respectively. As the grouse flew, the flankers would wave their flags strategically to startle the birds and funnel them towards the waiting guns.

Everything appeared to be in order. One last glance behind the butts to make sure that the two pickers-up and their dogs were well concealed in depressions amongst the heather. He turned once more to the front and checked his watch. It was two forty-five precisely, the appointed time to begin the fourth drive of the day. With great solemnity, he raised his horn to his lips and sounded the call to start the drive.

As the line of beaters moved slowly across the moor towards them, Settle began to grow anxious. The beaters had already covered several hundred yards but had not put up a single bird. He could hear the faint sound of flapping plastic as they swept their homemade flags back and forth. Suddenly there was a great commotion—a raucous cackling and clatter of wings. A dozen grouse had got up and were heading straight for the butts.

About two hundred yards out, half of them veered off to the right through the gap between the outermost flanker and the line of beaters, skimming over the heather like reddish brown cruise missiles. Settle cursed silently. The remaining birds flew directly over Mr. Dinsdale's shooting butt. Dinsdale rose up and fired, missing cleanly. He then turned and fired his remaining barrel at the retreating grouse. One of the birds appeared to wobble slightly then sailed on stiff wings for a hundred yards before going down. The pickers-up poked their heads above the heather to mark the location of the bird. "Bloody hell!" the old gamekeeper muttered. With shooting like that he'd be the laughingstock of his mates at the pub. A gamekeeper toiled on the moors—burning the old heather to promote new growth, poisoning competing bracken, spreading grit for the birds, and shooting foxes—for one reason only: to raise more grouse so that more could be shot. Every bird missed was a bird wasted, just like pouring a pint of the best Yorkshire bitter down the drain. And in the end, the head keeper was held to accounts.

The beaters were only about a hundred and fifty yards out now and getting within range of the guns. Settle was about to blow his horn—to signal, for reasons of safety, that the guns must now only shoot behind them—when all hell broke loose.

A large covey of grouse erupted with whirring wings from the heather, uttering their characteristic *go-beck-beck-beck*, as if they realized, too late, what was in store for them. The guns rose as one and started firing. In a few seconds a dozen birds were down, several of them beating death tattoos on the heather with their wings.

Harry Settle's attention, however, was elsewhere. He stared straight ahead, transfixed. Strange elflike figures were materializing on the moor before his very eyes. A longhaired sprite ran towards him, screaming something unintelligible. "Gawd Almighty," Settle whispered. Then he leapt to his feet, shouting amidst the fusillade, "Hold your bloody fire! Stop shooting!"

There was considerable confusion amongst the guns at first, but as the message was shouted down the line of butts, the shotgun blasts became sporadic, then, a few seconds later, ceased entirely. Several of the beaters had begun to run towards the butts. With a garbled scream, one of them stumbled and inexplicably vanished. Settle watched in numb disbelief. The longhaired creature—he realized now that it was a young woman—had stopped ten yards from him and produced a camera. She was snapping pictures of a wounded grouse that lay twitching spasmodically in a patch of dead bracken. She looked up at him. "Murderer," she said.

There were about half a dozen of them, another woman and three scruffy young men waving their arms and shouting at the guns. A fourth man, who appeared to be directing the operation, was recording the proceedings with a video camera.

Suddenly, something caught Settle's attention—one

of the beaters, Jack Long, the son of a local farmer, was closing in fast on the group of protesters. Uttering a blood-curdling cry perfected on the rugby pitch, he tackled the man with the video camera from behind, sending him and his equipment crashing to the ground. The other interlopers then piled onto Jack, just as the rest of the beaters arrived to join the melee. A wild scrum ensued with boots flying and bodies grappling in the heather. The dogs of the pickers-up strained at their leashes and barked excitedly. One of the women screamed as someone pulled her off the pile by her hair. There was derisive cheering from the butts. Utterly disgusted, Settle pointed his gun in the air and fired first one barrel then the other. The reports echoed across the moor like recriminating claps of thunder.

Judging by the reaction, he had made his point. The combatants disentangled themselves and scrambled to their feet looking embarrassed. Settle shook his head in amazement. A feeling of grudging respect crept over him as he realized how this ragtag group of guerillas had pulled it off. About thirty yards in front of the butts, a number of pits had been dug in the moor. The holes had been covered over with squares of plywood then camouflaged with cut blocks of heather. It was into one of these that the beater had fallen. The protesters had concealed themselves in their foxholes, waiting for the right moment to burst out and confront the guns. Settle looked them over with disgust on his face. "Well, what do you lot 'ave to say for yourselves?"

He heard a sharp voice behind him. "It's a bit late for that, Settle, don't you think?"

He turned and looked into the red face of his employer. "I'm sorry, Mr. Dinsdale, I—" He was interrupted by a commotion behind the butts. Mick Curtis, his assistant, was striding over with another man and four uniformed constables in tow. Settle felt like he'd been kicked in the gut.

"Good work, Curtis," Dinsdale said smartly, ignoring his head keeper. "I can see that I should have put you in charge from the start."

Mick, with an obsequious smirk, caught Settle's eye and said, "Thank you, Mr. Dinsdale."

"Hello, Dickie," said the man accompanying the constables.

"Jim, good to see you," Dinsdale replied heartily. "Shall we get on with it?"

The man smiled. "Always happy to help rid the moors of vermin."

He nodded at the ringleader, a bearded lad with matted dreadlocks, and then spoke to one of the constables. "Leave him with us."

"Yes, Mr. Braughton."

The policemen proceeded to handcuff the other protesters together and then herd them towards a waiting police van. One of the young men insisted on being dragged by his arm, cursing and kicking, over the rough ground. The young woman with the long hair was screaming obscenities.

Dinsdale addressed the assembled members of the shooting party. "I'm afraid there will be no more shooting today, but we'll make it up tomorrow. I suggest we all retire to the shooting box for a drink." He turned to

Curtis, once again ignoring Settle. "Mick, see to my father, would you?"

"Yes, Mr. Dinsdale."

"As for you, Settle, I'll deal with you later."

"Yes, sir," the gamekeeper mumbled, cringing with embarrassment.

As the guns and beaters and flankers and pickers-up with their dogs straggled back to the vehicles, Braughton turned to face his captive. "Hello, Stumpy."

The young man glared defiantly at him, saying nothing.

"You've heard of Stumpy Macfarlane, Dickie—the fearless tree-hugger."

"Sod off," Stumpy said.

Without warning, Dinsdale lunged, thrusting the butt end of his gun stock into the protester's solar plexus.

The young man gave an agonized grunt, then fell to the ground, gasping raspingly for air.

"Have a little respect for the inspector, lout," Dinsdale snarled.

Braughton shook his head sadly. "Wandering about on the moors can be hazardous to your health, Stumpy."

Stumpy looked up at Dinsdale, tears streaming from his eyes. "You son of a bitch!" he whispered hoarsely. "You'll pay for this."

"Uttering threats won't help you," Braughton said. "I am placing you under arrest for aggravated trespass and interfering with the lawful activity of others contrary to section sixty-eight of the Criminal Justice and Public Order Act. What have you got to say for yourself?"

Silence now, except for Stumpy's labored breathing.

"All right, get up and come along quietly—" The policeman felt a hand on his shoulder and heard Dinsdale's voice.

"That would be too easy, Jim. We need to teach the little bastard a lesson."

Braughton looked at Dinsdale. "I don't think that would be wise, Dickie."

Dinsdale smiled. "You needn't be involved. Just leave him to me."

Then he leveled his gun at Stumpy's head and pulled the trigger.

CHAPTER 1

The great house was quiet except for the creaking of floorboards beneath his bare feet and the faint knocking of pipes somewhere. Or the knocking of something else, he thought lasciviously. He experienced a familiar thrill of anticipation as he crept down the broad hall, his passage illuminated by a line of dim yellow lamps mounted on the wall, giving his soft features a sickly, jaundiced look. Between the lamps were hung a series of portraits.

He paused for a moment beneath the painting of his father. The eyes in the painting stared dully back at him, foreshadowing, he fancied, the dementia that lay ahead. He suppressed a shudder and tried to put the logical implication of this train of thinking out of his mind, consoling himself with the thought that Blackamoor would soon be his to do with as he pleased. His hand absently brushed against the hall table that stood against the wall beneath the portrait. He smiled unpleasantly. Nothing like the silky patina of a rosewood antique to put things in the proper perspective.

11

He continued down the hall. On his left ran the ornately carved balustrade that had, on more than one occasion, saved him from a drunken swan dive to the ballroom floor below. At the top of the grand staircase, he peered down into the gloom and frowned. He thought he'd heard something. The wind moaning on the moor, or was it just his imagination?

Suddenly he froze. There it was again—a sort of faint sighing, punctuated this time by a burst of feminine giggling. Hardly daring to believe his good fortune, he hurried to her door. He leaned against the wall for a moment to catch his breath. Then he pressed his ear to the thick panel and listened.

There was no mistake. The creaking of bedsprings and a muffled feminine voice, mostly unintelligible, excitedly urging her partner on, the occasional explicit instruction audible. God, she's a wanton bitch, he thought. She behaved as if the entire universe had been created solely for her pleasure. Talk about your Big Bang. He licked his lips—this was going to be good. He opened his dressing gown and pressed his body against the door, the smooth mahogany cool against his skin.

There was a man's voice now. Then the noises in the room ceased. There was a thump, followed by a soft footfall. He leapt back as if the door was electrified. Gathering his gown untidily around him, he flapped down the hall, trying not to rouse the entire household. He ducked into the first room on the left past the staircase. He shut the door behind him with more commotion than he'd intended and fell back against it, wheezing heavily. His interest in his stepsister's latest dalliance, not to put too fine a point on it, had flagged considerably.

At that moment, the woman's door opened and she stepped out into the hall. She looked to be in her twenties. She stood naked in the hallway like a vision of Venus, her appearance, unlike her voyeuristic stepbrother's, unsullied by the lurid light. There was something lying on the floor at her feet. She bent down and picked it up. A silk sash. She frowned and then turned back to the room. She knotted the sash loosely around her neck and tossed her long, dark hair in a seductive gesture. Her eyes, however, were cold. She looked at her companion and said, "There's nobody there. It must have been my imagination."

Frank Elger expertly fitted the final topstone into place then straightened slowly with an involuntary grunt. He surveyed the repaired section of drystone wall. "That's fixed it, Katie, lass," he said. "Good as new."

His daughter, who had been busy laying out the lunch things on the grass, looked up at him, concern in her eyes. "Here, Dad, I'll get you your beer."

Elger smiled. "That's music to my ears, lass." He gazed at her fondly. "If only your mother could see you now."

"Oh, Dad! Sit down and have your lunch."

He lowered himself stiffly onto the springy turf. Straightening his legs, he leaned back against the wall. He was sweating and the stone felt cool against his back. He took a swig from the long-necked bottle and sighed contentedly. "Soon be time to get t' hay in," he observed presently.

Katie nodded and handed him a sandwich. She perched herself on the wall. "You know, I think September is my favorite time of year here." Looking beyond her father, she scanned the vast expanse of moorland at the head of Brackendale with a naturalist's eye. Climbing steeply to the northern skyline that formed the dark backbone of the North York Moors, with the great valley of the Esk beyond, the moors were still glorious with the purple bloom of ling mixed with the greens and bronzes of crowberry and bilberry. But the deeper purple patches of bell heather were beginning to fade now, presaging the darker and colder times ahead. Below them, nearly hidden in a copse of alder beside a tiny gill was their gritstone farmhouse. Farther down the valley was a Lilliputian sprinkling of red pantile-roofed buildings—the village of Brackendale. Drystone walls, extending up the slopes on both sides of the dale and terminating just below the heather-clad tops, subdivided the green pastureland like the ribs of a great beast.

Katie experienced a sense of contentment, slightly tinged with melancholy, as she took in her surroundings. She only got home on weekends and holidays now, but she still felt like the luckiest person on earth. Like the purple haze of heather, however, she knew that it couldn't last forever. She looked down at her father. Short and wiry—as strong as a horse in his day—he now looked old and frail. His face had tightened into a frown, as if he were puzzling over something.

"What is it, Dad?"

"What? Ah, well, I was just wonderin' 'ow much t' beasts will fetch this year." He left the rest unsaid.

"Will there be enough, do you think?" she heard herself ask, her voice sounding hollow in her ears. She knew all too well that the price of sheep had recently plummeted.

He sighed. "I don't know, lass. Bugger's raised t' rent, 'asn't he?"

She flushed with anger. "It's just not fair! He has no right to—"

"Now, lass," her father admonished, "don't get started—'e owns this land and there's nowt we can do about it. With old Mr. Dinsdale it was different, but them days 'ave long gone."

She avoided his eyes. "Look, Dad, perhaps I can get a job with the National Park Authority and—"

"I'll 'ave none of that, Katie!" the old man exploded. "Tha'll be goin' back to university next month and I'll hear no more about it."

A troublesome wind had picked up. She followed the beck with her eyes from its confluence with the river, past their tiny farmstead, and up to the crest of the rigg above. Silhouetted against scudding clouds was a sprawling slate-roofed pile of gray stone with jutting chimneys and a dark-windowed facade. Lording over the dale and all its inhabitants. Katie felt a familiar loathing. It wasn't enough that he trampled on people's rights. She had suspected all along that he was trying to force them off their farm, even though it hadn't made any sense—no one could be a better tenant, a more conscientious steward of the land than her father—but now that she knew what he was up to, she hated him more than ever. She shivered, experiencing a sudden sense of foreboding. The farmers' shoot was tomorrow. She had half a mind not to go. She was afraid she might do something she'd later regret when confronted with their high-and-mighty landlord, but she knew her father would be disappointed. And she *had* promised Mrs. Settle she'd help with lunch.

She turned to her father with an odd expression on her face. "Don't worry, Dad. Everything will be all right. I promise."

Katie Elger looked out the window of the shooting box. The mist had settled over the moor once again, reducing the visibility to no more than a few yards. They'd only managed to get in one drive that morning, when the fog had briefly lifted. She didn't have much use for shooting and the so-called grouse economy for which the moors were managed primarily to produce shooting for the pleasure of the wealthy, but she didn't begrudge her father and the others a bit of fun. God knows there wasn't much of that these days. She had pitched in with the meal, and now, after lunch, she was helping Mrs. Settle with the washing up. The rest had gone back out for the afternoon shoot with hearty, if misplaced, optimism.

Isn't it just typical? Katie thought. The one day when the local farmers and workers who help out with the shooting all season were allowed to take a few birds for themselves. Compliments of Lord bloody Dickie. She grimaced. He'd no doubt be happy if the whole thing were called off, leaving more of his precious grouse for him and his paying customers. He'd brushed up against her at lunch, his breath rasping and reeking of alcohol, his intentions obvious. She'd almost kicked him in the balls. She would have if her father hadn't been there, she told herself.

"Hand me those cups, dear," Mrs. Settle said.

"Yes—yes, of course."

"Penny for your thoughts, lass," Mrs. Settle said, motherly concern showing in her face.

Katie hesitated. "I don't know, I suppose in a way I was wishing that things didn't have to change."

Mrs. Settle sighed. "I know what tha means, Katie, believe me."

There was something in her voice.

Then, without warning, the gamekeeper's wife began to sob convulsively.

Katie gathered her hands in hers. "What is it, Mrs. Settle?"

Tears streamed down her plump, white face. "It's no good, lass. There's nowt you can do about it."

"Tell me," Katie urged.

"It—it's my Harry. 'E's been sacked."

"What?" Katie asked incredulously.

"It's true. After forty years an' all." She began to sob again. "'E's 'elpin' out today only out of loyalty to t' others."

"There, there," Katie said reassuringly. "Sit down and I'll fix us a nice cup of tea, then you can tell me all about it."

Mrs. Settle wiped away her tears with a tea towel. "Thanks, lass. I've been keepin' it to myself for so long, it feels good to let it out."

The first sip of tea had a noticeably soothing effect on the gamekeeper's wife. She explained how Mr. Dinsdale had been furious about last month's protest on the Twelfth, as if there was anything Harry could have done about it. "Mr. Dinsdale told 'im that Mick Curtis would be head keeper beginnin' t'end of August. 'E said he'd let 'im stay on as Mick's assistant," she added indignantly.

"There's nowt Mick knows about keeperin' as my Harry hasn't taught 'im." Her expression suddenly darkened. "That one's always suckin' up to Mr. Dinsdale, tha knows!"

Katie was shocked at this news. There was no way in the world that old Harry Settle should be held responsible for the protest. "Mrs. Settle, I really don't know what to say. I'm so sorry." A burning sense of injustice welled up inside her. "It's just not fair!" she blurted out.

Mrs. Settle sighed. "Nay, lass, but is it fair that one man should own four thousand acres of land and everybody on it?"

Katie was mildly surprised by this expression of political consciousness from the gamekeeper's wife. "What are you going to do?" she asked in a quiet voice.

For the first time, there was a look of fear in Mrs. Settle's eyes. "I don't know, Katie, I honestly don't know. We've got nowt to call our own, really—just a few sticks of furniture. We've never owned our own home, never will at our time of life. We've allus lived at Rose Cottage, but tha knows t' house goes with t' job. We could live with Emma, I reckon, but it would kill Harry. 'E's such a proud man." She dabbed at her eyes with the towel.

Katie was angry now. She was thinking about her father, his thin face etched with worry. "There must be something we can do!" she protested.

Mrs. Settle shook her head slowly. "Not so long as *'e's* around."

Katie Elger shivered convulsively. The mist gathered around her like the ghosts of her childhood as she followed the rough track that led over the blackened wasteland of burnt heather to the grouse butts on East Moor. There had been times as a young girl when she had been caught out on the moor above Dale End Farm when the fog set in. It was strange, but she hadn't been afraid then, imagining that she was Cathy, lost on the moor between Thrushcross Grange and Wuthering Heights, or an angel dancing amongst the silver clouds of heaven. Today, however, she felt cold and damp and utterly alone. And try as she might, she was unable to suppress a palpable feeling of dread. It was midafternoon, but it might as well have been midnight in the dead of a nuclear winter.

She had set out from the shooting box with a flask of tea for her father on a journey that would normally have taken less then ten minutes. But the farther she walked, the more difficult it became to pick out the muddy ruts, and after twenty minutes she found herself up to the tops of her Wellies in a bog. She could barely see the hand in front of her face and didn't have the slightest clue where she was. She tried not to worry. After all, she reassured herself, if she went too far to the east she'd eventually end up in Rosedale; too far west and she'd hit Blackamoor Rigg Road. She carefully retraced her steps until she was on firm ground again. She thought about calling out—assuming she hadn't wandered too far off course, she should be getting fairly close to the butts—but she was too embarrassed to admit to the others that she had gotten lost.

She set out once more, bearing right to skirt the patch of wet ground, her boots rustling against the blackened stalks of heather. The ground began to rise and as she climbed she had the impression that the mist was beginning to thin. Suddenly she stopped. What was that just then? She listened intently. There was nothing but the sound of her breathing, muffled in the stillness as if she were enclosed in a translucent white chrysalis. She was sure that she'd heard something, a faint groaning sound. She chided herself (letting her imagination get the better of her like that!) and started walking again. She could visualize the gleam in her father's eye when she told him about her little adventure—

There it was again! There was no doubt about it this time. An unintelligible muttering, then a horrible gurgling sound. It seemed very close. Now she was truly afraid.

A voice cried out. Then, before she could react, a gunshot boomed over the moor; a second later there was another loud report. Katie began to run towards the sound, stumbling over the uneven ground, frantically calling out for her father. Just ahead, the dark shape of a shooting butt and a figure loomed in the mist. She stopped short and began to walk slowly towards the figure, as if in a trance. She was very close now. It spoke to her in a halting voice.

"Must get help . . . still time if we hurry . . ."

She recognized Mick Curtis, his face white, his eyes wide and staring.

Her stomach knotted. "What's wrong? What is it?" she asked mechanically. It was as if somebody else were speaking.

His mouth moved, but he seemed unable to make a sound. He raised his arm and pointed at the butt.

From her vantage point, Katie could see only a gray, lichen-stained wall. She approached the gamekeeper with a morbid sense of curiosity. A shotgun lay on the ground at his feet. She looked inside the butt and gasped.

There, lying facedown on the short-cropped grass was a man. As Katie stared, the body jerked spasmodically. It smelled like someone had been sick. "We must turn him over on his back," she said slowly, remembering her first aid.

Curtis did not move.

She looked at him. "I'll need your help," she said.

There was no response.

She slowly approached the prostrate form, took a deep breath, and knelt down beside him. A shock of recognition surged through her—it was Dickie Dinsdale. She spoke to him, but there was no response. She was about to feel for a pulse when a movement in the corner of the butt caught her eye.

It was twisting and coiling and lashing back and forth like a thick yellow rope, all frayed and dripping red at the end. She stared at it incomprehensibly. At some level of consciousness, she could hear a commotion of boots and voices behind her. She slowly got to her feet and backed away. She stumbled, nearly bumping into Curtis. She turned and stared at him. With a strangled cry, he fell to his knees and began to vomit.

She stared out the kitchen window through her own insubstantial reflection into the darkness. She was aware of the clock in the sitting room ticking loudly. She turned to look at her father, her face expressionless. "That's the way it happened, Dad. It was awful."

Frank Elger nodded slowly, sucking with studied deliberation on his pipe.

CHAPTER 2

Powell sat alone in his study. A green-shaded lamp spilled a pool of light onto the desk. He poured himself another drink and inserted a disk into the CD player. Diana Krall this time, her voice smooth and smoky like the Scotch. He lit a cigarette. His movements were slow and measured, as if he were performing the task for the first time. He exhaled slowly. Funny thing, life. Like a drunk staggering past a street lamp—a brief interval of illumination before being swallowed up again by the darkness. The existential equivalent of Warhol's fifteen minutes.

He tried to recall the time when everything seemed possible, even happiness. His university days, the army, then marriage and the blur of the years. His sons grown now and so many things left undone and unsaid. He heard the faint slamming of a door upstairs. Marion going to bed. Alone. He swore without venom. He wondered how it had come to this, a prospect as unequivocal as a flat gray sky.

He drained his glass and set it aside. A battered brown leather gun case lay on the side of the desk. He placed it in front of him, released the brass locks, and flipped back the top. He removed the barrels from their baize-lined compartment, the cool touch of steel and the sweet, oily smell oddly soothing. He unfastened the fore-end from the underside of the barrels and placed it on the desk. Then, transferring the tubes to his left hand and gripping the finely checkered wrist of the stock in his right, he pushed the top lever over with his thumb and carefully fitted the hook of the front barrel lump onto the hinge pin of the action. He closed the gun and released the top lever to lock it. He snapped the fore-end back into place to complete the operation.

When he was satisfied that all was in order, he broke open the action of the shotgun and lay it on its case. The intricately engraved action body glowed in the lamplight with faint traces of hardening colors, a paisley of swirling scroll work. The dark walnut stock was grainy and figured like a man's face. A masterpiece of elegance and efficiency bequeathed to him by craftsmen long dead. There was some comfort in that, he supposed.

He reached down and lifted a canvas cartridge bag from the bottom drawer and placed it on the cracked leather surface of the desk. He sat motionless for several minutes. Eventually he stirred, as if coming to a decision.

There would be time enough to pack his things in the morning. Right now another glass of the frim fram sauce with Ms. Krall, then lurch into unconsciousness past, one hoped, another lamppost. He dismantled the gun and returned it to its case.

* * *

The next morning, a brief encounter with Marion at breakfast.

"What time did you come to bed?" she asked.

He avoided her eye. "Er, well, I don't remember exactly. I was getting my kit organized."

She seemed about to say something then apparently changed her mind. "There's a letter from Peter," she said. "It's on the table."

Powell poured himself a cup of coffee. He prayed it wasn't decaf. He sat down and opened the letter. "He seems to be settling in all right," he said presently. "I always thought Canadians were a boring lot, but that only applies to the male of the species, apparently. I wonder how he finds the time to study."

"You always managed."

"Look where it got me," Powell rejoined.

She looked at him with an odd expression. "You might have done worse." She joined him at the table, bearing a rack of toast and a pot of marmalade. "I think you're just jealous. The experience will do him good."

He despaired at times that his elder son was so much like himself; David, the practical one, was definitely his mother's son. It was hard to believe—Peter off to university in Canada and David thinking about following him over next year. Where had the time gone? As the caffeine revitalized his brain cells, it occurred to him that his mood these days seemed to be pervaded by a general sense of summer winding down.

"When are you leaving?" Marion was asking.

He shrugged. "I've got to stop by the office first. I'm hoping to get away by noon."

She smiled crookedly. "Say hello to Alex for me."

Powell grunted.

She looked at him, a flicker of concern in her eyes. "Do try and enjoy yourself, Erse."

"What's that supposed to mean?"

"Well, your last sporting expedition with Alex wasn't much of a holiday, was it?"

"I didn't exactly plan it that way," he said in a flat voice.

She realized she was treading on dangerous ground. "I know."

They ate their breakfast in silence.

"We need to talk about next year," Marion said eventually.

"Yes?"

"My sabbatical."

"What about it?"

"You know I'd like to get back into the field. I mean, I haven't been out of the classroom for years." She hesitated. "I've had an offer from that chap I met at the conference last spring, a chance to spend a year at the University of British Columbia, starting next September. I've always had an interest in North American Native culture and, well, it's a wonderful opportunity."

"Really?" he said stiffly.

"Can't we at least talk about it?"

"What's there to talk about? It sounds like you've already made up your mind."

She brushed a wisp of blonde hair from her forehead in a gesture of exasperation. "I haven't, actually."

There was an awkward interval during which neither of them spoke.

Powell looked at her. What was there to say after all

these years? "Perhaps it's best. As you say, it's a chance in a lifetime, and you'll be able to keep tabs on the boys."

"What about you?"

"I'll manage."

"You could come out for your holidays. It would do you good."

"Yes, right." Not with a bang, but a whimper, he thought. He rose abruptly from the table. "Say good-bye to David for me, would you?"

A few minutes later she heard him go out the front door. She stirred her coffee mechanically. "Good-bye," she said quietly.

From the window of Powell's office at New Scotland Yard, the Thames, cloaked in early morning mist, looked like a giant cotton wool snake slithering along Victoria Embankment. Detective-Sergeant Bill Black sat across the desk from him, looking slightly queasy.

"What's up, Bill?"

"You mean you haven't heard?"

"Heard what?"

"It's Merriman, sir. He's going for it—" Black gulped "—the Full bloody Monty."

Powell groaned. "Good Christ."

Sir Richard Conway, Commissioner of the Metropolitan Police Service and basically a decent chap, had recently announced his retirement. There had followed the usual flurry of maneuvering by the assistant commissioners who were in line for the job, with one notable exception: Powell's supervisor, nemesis, and archbureaucrat, Sir Henry Merriman. Sir Henry had announced early his intention to remain above the fray, being content, as he put it, to continue in a "hands-on" role. (But hands on *what*? Powell had wondered at the time.) It was obvious now that the whole thing had simply been a ploy to keep the competition off balance before throwing his hat in the ring.

"You don't think he's got a shot at it do you?" Black asked, a plaintive I-believe-in-fairies note in his gruff voice.

"This is it, then." Powell said to no one in particular. Then a lengthy silence. Eventually he spoke. "Look at the bright side, Bill. With Merriman at the helm, we won't have to bother ourselves with sex killings or major drug deals anymore—we'll be able to devote our full attention to his Corporate Sponsorship Initiative."

Sergeant Black uttered an uncharacteristic expletive.

Powell was referring to Merriman's latest brainchild, a scheme whereby private companies—an organization representing car hire-purchase firms, for instance—could "invest" in the salaries of police officers on a basis determined by the value of stolen goods recovered. The possibilities were both endless and mind numbing—rent-a-cops stumbling over bodies in the street in their haste to recover the property of their corporate masters. Powell looked out the window at a watery blue sky hovering ethereally above the fog. He turned again to Black. "You'll hold the fort while I'm away?"

The stocky sergeant smiled. "Of course, Mr. Powell. And good luck up in Scotland. I used to do a bit of shooting myself as a lad. Rabbits, mostly, and the odd pheasant when we could get permission. Never grouse, of course."

Powell, uncomfortable with class distinctions of any

kind, implied or otherwise, felt a little self-conscious. "Well, it's just a bit of walked-up shooting Alex has organized. Nothing too elaborate."

Black was grinning now. From what he knew of Mr. Powell and his mate, Chief Inspector Alex Barrett of Inverness, there would no doubt be a spirited competition for the best shot and biggest bag. "Give my regards to Mr. Barrett, sir."

"I'll do that—" The telephone on his desk began to beep insistently. He picked up the receiver. "Powell," he barked. His expression darkened. "Right." He slammed down the phone. "It's Merriman. He wants to see me after lunch."

Sergeant Black sympathized with his superior, but he realized that there was nothing he could say.

Powell decided to make the best use of his time before his meeting with Sir Henry by indulging in an unplanned pleasure. He took the tube to Goodge Street station and strolled briskly amongst the lunch-hour bustle to his destination in Charlotte Street. Just ahead, sandwiched between a Greek kebab house and an American-style pizza joint, he could see the familiar green awning below the impressionistic sign suggesting the jagged peaks of the high Karakoram: K2 TANDOORI RESTAURANT.

The restaurant was fairly busy; the two waiters on duty rushed back and forth, carrying trays laden with a variety of steaming and fragrant dishes. Powell's sense of anticipation, however, was tempered somewhat by the discovery that his usual table near the window was taken. Rashid Jamal, the energetic proprietor, was over in a flash. "Erskine, my dear fellow. This is a surprise. I wasn't expecting you back for a week."

Powell smiled sourly. "At the rate I'm going, I may never get away."

"I am sorry about your table, my friend, but wait—there is one over there, in the corner . . ." There was a look of concern in Rashid's dark eyes.

"Perfect. It's close to the bar."

"I'll bring you one of your usual, then?"

"Only if you'll join me—if you're not too busy, that is."

Rashid grinned. "I'm never too busy for you, my friend."

A few minutes later they were chatting over their drinks, a lager for Powell, an orange squash for his host. "Any developments on the home front?" Powell inquired neutrally.

Rashid sighed. "They will not listen to reason, my friend—they are determined to get married. It is very awkward. We come from two very different traditions and it will be difficult, but what can I say?" He shrugged sadly. "You know these modern young people as well as I do. They will not listen to their parents, or to anyone else, for that matter." He looked at Powell, his dark eyes moist. "Nindi and I want only for them to be happy."

A few months ago, Rashid's eldest son, Ziad, had fallen in love with a Hindu girl. Powell had gathered that both Rashid and his wife, Nindi, were fond of the young woman but were concerned about their son marrying outside of their community. It seemed, however, that Ziad and his sweetheart were a determined young couple. Powell wondered how he would feel if he were in

Rashid's shoes. "If they love each other, I'm sure they will be very happy." He tried to sound reassuring.

"I hope you are right, Erskine. Love can make ordinary people do the strangest bloody things." He sighed sadly. "As my dear mother used to say, 'Life without love is like meat without *masala*.'" He looked at Powell with a questioning expression on his face. "And what about you, my friend?"

"Me? Oh, fine—no complaints," Powell replied offhandedly. "We got a letter from Peter this morning; he seems to be, er, getting into the swing of things at university."

Rashid grinned. "He is a bright boy, is he not? A chip off the old block?" He noted Powell's rueful expression. "Now, then," he continued briskly, sensitive as always to his friend's mood, "how would you like today's special *thali* to fortify you for the northern climes?"

"Rashid, I think I've died and gone to heaven."

When he got back to the Yard, Powell cleared off his desk, generously bequeathed a box of files to Detective-Sergeant Black, and then, exuding a cloud of garlic and fenugreek, went upstairs to see Merriman. Nothing like making a powerful impression on one's superior to further the career.

Sir Henry Merriman, Assistant Commissioner of the Metropolitan Police Service, looked up from the single blue file folder on his desk. "Ah, Powell," he said with obvious disinterest. "Sit down." He turned his attention back to the docket and continued reading.

Powell fixed his attention on Merriman's transplanted and immaculately coiffed hair. Having been precociously knighted for hatching various politically astute but hare-brained schemes, such as the Metropolitan Police Green Plan, Sir Henry epitomized for Powell everything that was wrong with the police bureaucracy—the triumph of expediency over integrity.

Eventually Merriman looked up and drawled, "Bit of trouble at t' mill, apparently."

"I beg your pardon?"

"There's been a suspicious death in Yorkshire."

Powell felt his stomach knot.

"I imagine you've heard of Ronnie Dinsdale."

Powell refused to bite.

"The owner and former managing director of Dinsdale's, the supermarket chain. Last week his son, Richard—known as Dickie—was found dead in a grouse butt on the Dinsdale estate in the North York Moors."

"What's it got to do with me?" Powell said evenly.

Merriman ignored him, sucking in his breath in an affected manner. "The coroner has been unable to come to a conclusion as to the precise cause of death and the locals suspect foul play—"

"I'm starting my holiday today," Powell interjected.

"I'm afraid you'll have to change your plans, old boy. This one is right up your alley." He smiled coldly. "You being a shooting man . . ."

Powell made a heroic effort to control himself. Merriman was sticking one up his alley all right. His mind raced as he considered his options.

"It's a bit ticklish, you see," Merriman continued. "You'll never guess who was found skulking about the estate the day before Dinsdale's death . . ." A farcical pause for effect. "Stumpy Macfarlane, the environmental activist—you must have read about him. Spends his time parading old tree stumps through the streets of London to protest the logging of the world's rain forests and generally obstructing progress."

This from the architect of the Met's Green Plan, thought Powell.

Turning once more to the file on his desk, Merriman absently rubbed his prominent chin, a feature oddly enough not evident in an early photograph of him with his graduating class of police cadets that used to hang on the wall in the Metropolitan Police Training Centre. There he was, looking self-important in the back row, weak chinned and starting to go bald. One day the photograph had mysteriously disappeared, and ever since, the authenticity of Merriman's various body parts had been the subject of much ribald speculation amongst the rank and file.

"On August twelfth of this year," Merriman droned on, "Macfarlane organized a group of antis to protest the opening day of grouse shooting on Dinsdale's estate. It seems that things got a bit out of hand and old Stumpy sustained a few bumps and bruises during the proceedings."

"According to the newspaper reports, somebody beat the hell out of him," Powell commented, against his better judgment.

Merriman glared at him. "In any case, Macfarlane brought assault charges against the late young Mr. Dinsdale as well as the local police. As there could be a perception that the locals have an ax to grind, the chief constable has asked for our assistance"—here, a steely smile—"and I've decided to assign you to the case."

"Can't someone else do it?" Powell was getting desperate now.

"I want *you* to do it." Merriman said, obviously enjoying himself.

"You're aware that I've already arranged my holiday?"

"Bad luck, old man."

"If I refuse?"

Merriman leaned back in his chair and regarded Powell dispassionately. "I'll soon have the top job in the firm. Jerk me around and I'll put you in charge of stationery procurement."

"You really are an utterly contemptible prick."

Merriman smiled. "I'll ignore that for the time being. I don't like you, Powell, never have. But you're useful to me. For some reason, which I am at a loss to understand, you seem to have a talent for this sort of thing. As long as you continue to be useful, I'll keep you in the field." He smirked. "I know you better than you know yourself. You're dedicated to the job—obsessively so, some might say." His expression hardened. "So, you see, you need me more than I need you. And, oh, yes, there's one more thing: I want you to take Detective-Sergeant Evans along with you. She could use the field experience." He smiled unpleasantly. "I've got plans for her. We need more women in positions of authority. And I imagine with her along you'll be spending less time in the pub."

No bloody doubt, Powell thought with a sinking feeling. "Will there be anything else?" he said, carefully controlling his voice. He'd be buggered if he'd give Merriman the satisfaction of seeing how furious he was.

"Your contact in Northallerton is Superintendent Cartwright . . ."

Powell was already on his way out the door of Merriman's office. He slammed it behind him, his face burning.

CHAPTER 3

After explaining the situation to a grumbling Sergeant Black, who was clearly miffed at being passed over for Evans, Powell left a brief message for Marion on their answering machine. He then rang up Barrett to break the news. Before he could say anything, Barrett launched into a paean to the pleasures of grouse shooting: "Ah, the bracing moorland air, comely lasses beating through the heather, the clatter of wings over the butts, the smell of cordite, and the merry yipping of spaniels. And later, after a wee dram or two in front of the fire, a climax of roasted fowl washed down with a bottle of good claret— I can't tell you how much I've been looking forward to this week, Erskine," he expounded heartily. "Brings back memories of my lost youth."

A number of things went through Powell's mind (he didn't have the heart to interrupt) as he listened to Barrett wax eloquently, as only a Scotsman could, about his national bird. First off, driven grouse shooting, of the type described by Barrett, was an elitist and expensive pursuit. From what he knew of his friend's middle-class background, he thought it unlikely that he'd have had the means to pursue the sport. However, Barrett, who was blind in his right eye, had once let slip that a stray pellet taken while grouse shooting as a lad was the cause of it. Perhaps he'd preferred his grouse poached in those days, Powell speculated.

When Barrett eventually paused to take a breath, Powell interjected abruptly, "There's been a change of plans, Alex. I can't come. I'm sorry." The direct approach was usually best with Barrett.

An ominous silence followed on the other end of the line, an imagined lit fuse to be followed at any moment by an explosion of expletives. The seconds ticked by. Then Barrett spoke in a surprisingly measured voice. "You'd better explain yourself."

Powell did his best, complete with an unsolicited diatribe about Merriman. "And that's not the worst of it," he concluded glumly. "I'll be right in the middle of the best grouse-shooting moors in Yorkshire—bloody working!"

This seemed to catch Barrett's attention. "Oh, aye?" Then a significant pause. "What about the lassie?"

"Sarah Evans?" Powell shrugged. "She's all right. Young, bright, ambitious. Not exactly my choice for a traveling companion, though."

"Well, not to worry, Erskine," Barrett said brightly. "I'll just have to carry on without you. I've got the time booked off anyway, and I know a lassie who might enjoy a wee taste of the, em, sporting life."

No bloody doubt, Powell thought, feeling a bit put out.

"And Erskine . . ."

Powell steeled himself. "Yes."

"You owe me. You can put me up the next time I come down to London."

"Great," Powell replied unconvincingly. He was hardly in a position to object.

Several hours later, Powell left the A64 on the outskirts of York and pulled into a filling station for some petrol. Before leaving the Yard, he had rung Superintendent Cartwright in Northallerton and suggested that they meet at the police station in Malton the day after tomorrow, giving him a day to poke around the moors first. He had then spoken with Detective-Sergeant Evans, who planned to follow in a company car tomorrow.

After paying the attendant, he parked his battered green Triumph beside a shiny red VW van in front of the adjoining transport cafe and went in for a cup of coffee. There was a young couple in the next booth: the lad with bright orange hair in a moth-eaten jersey, and his waifish, nose-ringed companion looking distinctly unhappy. (A lover's tiff? Powell wondered.) The coffee was undrinkable, but the spirited exchange at the counter between the only other customer—a lorry driver—and the couple who owned the place more than made up for it. From what Powell was able to gather, the cafe had once been a favorite stop for long-distance lorry drivers, including, apparently, this fellow. It had recently been taken over by the couple, who had apparently decided to improve the tone of the place. Powell had noticed that quiche and "fresh garden greens" figured prominently on the menu, rather than the egg and chips and stodgy meat pies that one would normally expect in such an establishment. He reckoned that the pastel salmon-and-avocado decor was a dead giveaway.

The lorry driver was becoming increasingly agitated as he complained about the minuscule order of chips served up with the pale, crescent-shaped object (which might well have been the spinach and feta croissant) that lay beside a sprig of something green on the stark landscape of his plate. His face grew redder and redder as the husband foolishly went on about the dire consequences of dietary animal fat. Powell was becoming concerned that he would have to intervene to prevent an assault, when the wife interjected irritably, "For God's sake, Jim. Give him some more frigging chips!"

Her husband flushed then disappeared through the swinging doors into the kitchen.

"Tha's better," the lorry driver grunted.

The pinched-looking woman rolled her eyes, picked up the coffee pot, and began to walk towards Powell. He raised his hand politely. "No, thank you, I've heard that excessive caffeine has a tendency to inflame the baser passions."

The young man in the next booth sniggered.

After a late breakfast at his hotel in York, Powell continued on to Malton, where he was to meet Sarah Evans the following morning, then north on the A169. At Pickering, he turned west on the A170, and after a short drive through green and pleasant farmland, he was wheeling his car into the roundabout at Kirkbymoorside, a small market town situated, not surprisingly, on the edge of the North York Moors. The cobble-edged Market Place was lined with quaint village shops and a number of hotels that had once been coaching inns in the days when the town was on the main road from Thirsk to Scarborough. The old stable yards, access to which was obtained through narrow archways, had been converted to car parks. There was even a Chinese restaurant, he noticed, but (here, a twinge of disappointment) not a curry house in sight. He drove past tidy red-roofed houses into the open countryside, Long John Baldry blaring on the tape player. It was a glorious morning with the top down and the wind in his face, the throb of the TR4's engine and just a nip of autumn in the air. He felt as if he'd been reincarnated, the normal routine fading from his consciousness like the dim memory of a past, slightly unsavory life.

The road rose gradually as he left Kirkbymoorside and the gentle valley of the River Rye behind. He had learned from a guidebook that he'd picked up in Charing Cross Road the day before that the North York Moors National Park was essentially an uplifted plateau, broken along the southern edge by an irregular line of limestone scarps, through which a number of south-flowing streams cut channels to the River Rye. The resulting headlands, called "nab ends" by the locals, gazed stonily northward like sphinxes. Thus, as he climbed almost imperceptibly out of the Vale of Pickering into the Tabular Hills, the ground suddenly fell away, revealing a "surprise view." And few were more spectacular than the view from the village of Farnmoor, through which Powell now drove.

At the edge of the village, where the road began its plunge to the valley bottom, he was treated to a most fetching prospect: the green sweep of lower Brackendale, sheep-dotted fields, crisscrossed by drystone walls, giving way on the tops to vast tracts of brown-and-green moorland, tinged with purple, as far as the eye could see. There wasn't a cloud in the sky and the bracing air enlivened his senses. Directly below was a cluster of farm buildings set on the wooded banks of the River Merlin.

He started down the steep, narrow road, hugging the inside bank and keeping his eye out for places to pull off in the event of oncoming traffic. He reached the bottom of the hill without mishap, turned up the West Daleside Road, and drove for about a mile until he came to the picturesque hamlet of Brackendale. The village consisted of a row of tidy stone houses, each with its garden sloping down to the river, a general village shop, a teahouse, and a promising-looking pub and inn called the Lion and Hippo. Powell searched his memory for more guidebook lore and recalled that in the early 1800s, workmen quarrying stone for a road at Kirkdale Cave, not far from Kirkbymoorside, had uncovered the ancient bones of animals, including tigers, rhinoceroses, and hyenas—the source, one presumed, of the pub's intriguing name. Pleasant, Powell imagined, to contemplate over a pint a time when lions roared in the forests of Yorkshire and hippos basked in the warm waters of Ryedale.

Powell drove slowly through the village. Just past the pub, a stocky gray-haired man stood on a white-painted bridge over the beck, staring into the gravelly shallows. A woman, who seemed to be waiting for him, stood on the far bank with a Labrador retriever. Powell pulled off to the side of the road and unfolded his Ordnance Survey map. Beyond the village the road crossed over the river and climbed steeply to the east to the top of Blackamoor Rigg, the narrow ridge of moorland between Brackendale and Rosedale. Marked on the map at several locations were lines of dots, perpendicular to the axis of the ridge, labeled GROUSE BUTTS. And there, dead center on the moor, was a tiny rectangle with the notation BLACKAMOOR HALL. The country seat of Ronnie Dinsdale, the supermarket magnate. Powell felt the familiar thrill of anticipation that signified the start of a new case, forgetting for the moment the circumstances that had brought him there.

He returned the map to the glove box, eased the car into gear, and set out for Blackamoor Rigg. The road followed the river for half a mile or so, crossed over, then began the steep climb up to the skyline ridge. At the foot of the incline, a road branched off, continuing northward along the east side of the river, a faded fingerpost indicating the way to Dale End Farm. Powell geared down and urged his car up the 20 percent grade. Near the top he had to pull over onto the verge beside a stone-walled sheep enclosure to let a car coming down the hill pass by.

The transition from pasture to heather was sudden and dramatic as the road climbed up onto Blackamoor Rigg. Powell turned north on the main road and pulled off to the side to get his bearings. The sun had disappeared behind a cloud and Powell felt a sudden chill. In contrast to his earlier view of the sunlit tops, the vast expanse of moorland now seemed desolate and slightly menacing. The ribbon of road linking Eskdale and Ryedale disappeared over the horizon, and just ahead, perched dramatically on a rock promontory overlooking upper Brackendale, stood a large house. Blackamoor

Hall, no doubt. Off to the west, he could see the green fields of Farndale in the distance, and to his right the moor dropped off gradually into Rosedale. Powell glanced at his watch—it was ten past one—and wondered what he should do next. There was no point in putting in an appearance at Blackamoor Hall until he had been fully briefed, and that wasn't going to happen until tomorrow morning when he met with Sarah Evans and the locals in Malton. Hardy black-faced sheep grazed at the edge of the road and a curlew cried persistently, as if urging him to make a decision. His stomach grumbled and his thoughts suddenly turned tropical. The Lion and Hippo was, after all, the local pub, and in his long experience as a policeman (he reminded himself, as if by way of rationalization) he had learned that there was no better source of local information. He gunned the motor, spun the little roadster around, and plunged back down into Brackendale.

Except for a man with black hair slicked neatly back, who was behind the bar reading the *Ryedale Times* when Powell walked in, the Lion and Hippo was deserted.

The man looked up. He seemed mildly surprised to be interrupted by a customer. "Afternoon, sir," he remarked pleasantly. "What'll it be?"

Powell sat down at the bar and surveyed the row of hand pulls. "A pint of Tetley's, please."

The man slowly pumped the pint glass full of bitter, allowing an alarming quantity of the creamy beer to overflow into the drain. Then he set the glass on the bar and examined it critically. When the foam had settled, he topped it up and placed it in front of Powell. "We like a good head up North," he said pointedly, implying that the same couldn't be said down South. "That'll be one pound fifty-five."

Powell paid and then raised his glass. "Cheers." He took an appreciative sip. "You the landlord?"

The man nodded. "Robert Walker, at your service."

Powell quickly sized up the fellow and decided to take his chances. He was hoping that he would find in the publican a knowledgeable but reasonably objective observer who could provide some useful background information. "I'd be interested in your thoughts about what happened to Dickie Dinsdale," he said.

Walker looked wary. "What's your interest in it?"

Powell handed him his card.

The landlord whistled softly. "I see. It's difficult to know where to begin, Chief Superintendent." He hesitated for an instant. "One doesn't like to speak ill of the dead, but I suppose it's safe to say that Dickie Dinsdale wasn't very popular in these parts. It was different with his father. Old Ronnie Dinsdale is well respected in the dale. He was fair with his employees and tenants and didn't put on any airs. When he got sick—he's got Alzheimer's, or something like it—he handed over the running of his supermarket business, as well as the estate, to Dickie. Both enterprises have been on the skids ever since."

"Do you know how Dickie died?"

"They say he was bit by a bloody adder during the farmers' shoot last Saturday."

Powell raised an eyebrow. Merriman hadn't said anything about an adder. He wondered if he had come all this way for nothing.

"There's quite a few of them round the moors," Walker volunteered, "but the bite's not usually fatal." He wiped the surface of the bar with a towel. "Perhaps Dinsdale had a weak constitution," he added, as if by way of an afterthought.

Powell remembered that Stumpy Macfarlane, the environmental activist with whom Dinsdale had a previous well-publicized confrontation, had been seen in the neighborhood around the time of Dinsdale's death. He mentioned this to Walker.

"I wouldn't know about that," the landlord said stiffly. "Blokes like him should learn to mind their own business."

A noncommittal grunt from Powell. Walker was obviously not a supporter of the Hunt Saboteurs Association. He took in his surroundings—the cozy snug to the left of the bar, the stone hearth and blackened oak beams, the walls done tastefully in dark green and hung with prints depicting Yorkshire's past cricketing glory. He took another sip of bitter. He had already decided that the Lion and Hippo would make an ideal base of operations. Centrally located and undoubtedly the hub of social life in the dale—not to mention a recommendation in the CAMRA *Good Beer Guide*. He inquired about a room.

Walker smiled thinly. "You can have your pick. The daffodil season in the spring and the summer months are our busy times," he explained. "We don't get many visitors to the park this time of year, except for a few who come for the shooting, but, well, I don't expect there'll be any more shooting this year."

Something suddenly occurred to Powell. "I'd better

book a room for my assistant, as well. She'll be joining me tomorrow."

Walker shrugged. "The more the merrier." He resumed polishing the bar. "Tell me, Chief Superintendent—that is, if you don't mind me asking—do the police think Dinsdale's death might not have been an accident?"

Powell eyed him speculatively. "Too early to tell, I expect."

Walker shifted on his feet. "I mean, well, I shouldn't think they'd bring someone up all the way from London . . ." He left the rest unsaid.

Powell sighed. "That," he said, "is a long story." He climbed off his stool. "I'll get my things."

As Powell was returning with his bag and gun case (which he'd brought along just in case), a woman came into the entrance hall from a room off to the right. From the computer and clutter of papers visible behind her, this room appeared to be the office. There was a framed picture of an older couple on the desk. "I'm Emma Walker," she said, her tone pleasant but businesslike.

Powell introduced himself.

"Robert has told me all about you," she volunteered.

Powell smiled. "Not everything, I hope, Mrs. Walker."

"I've put you in Number Three. It's our best room. Second one on your left at the top of the stairs. Loo's at the end of the hall. I'll put your colleague in Number Two, next door to you."

She was tall, attractive in an austere sort of way, with a certain preoccupied air that was hard to pin down. "We do pub grub next door and breakfast and dinner in the dining room," she said.

"I'd like to spend the rest of the afternoon exploring

the dale. Could you do me some sandwiches to take along?"

"Of course. Would ham and cheese be all right?"

Powell thanked her and started up the stairs.

He drove up past Dale End Farm and stopped to enjoy his lunch on a grassy bank beside the beck and watch the tiny yellow trout leaping in the spume. He returned by way of the East Daleside Road to the foot of Farnmoor Bank where he had started out that morning, thus completing his circle tour of Brackendale. When he got back to the Lion and Hippo, the pub was populated with about a dozen of its regular patrons, who eyed him suspiciously over their glasses. Whether this was traditional northern reserve or related to the fact that he was a policeman (which everyone in the village undoubtedly knew by now), Powell was unsure. He chatted with Walker about this and that, attempting to glean as much information as he could without appearing to be prying. He eventually managed to break the ice with a couple of the locals sitting beside him at the bar—one was the owner of the local garage and the other a retired farmer— and got an earful about Dickie Dinsdale. Several pints of best Yorkshire bitter and a traditional roast beef dinner later, Powell made his way up to his room and went to bed early. He dreamt that Merriman had him stuffed and mounted and put on display in the Millennium Dome as an early relic in Sir Henry's much vaunted Evolution of British Policing exhibit.

CHAPTER 4

Powell was not exactly looking forward to his meeting
with the local police that morning. He knew that he
would be regarded as an interloper, a trespasser on the
local patch. And as he turned onto the Old Malton Road,
he realized that in a curious way he regarded Detective-
Sergeant Sarah Evans in much the same light. He located the police station without difficulty and pulled into
the car park. She was waiting for him in a black Vauxhall.
She got out of the car to greet him.

"Mr. Powell," she said briskly.

"Evans," Powell acknowledged. "Have a pleasant trip?"

"Yes, sir."

It struck Powell for the first time, seeing her out of
her natural habitat at the Yard, that she was quite attractive. Fairly tall with short blonde hair combed off her
forehead, looking casual in a pair of jeans and an Arran
jumper. Her expression, however, was formal. "What do
you know about this business?" he asked, testing the
waters.

She shrugged lightly. "Only what I was able to get from Bill Black, which wasn't much."

"Didn't Merriman talk to you?"

"Merriman?" She seemed surprised. "No, sir, I ..." She hesitated. "You didn't pick me for this job, did you?"

Powell looked at her. "No, Evans, I didn't." Then he smiled. "Nor, I expect, would you pick me, if you had any say in the matter. But it looks like we're stuck with each other."

"Yes, sir." Chilly.

Powell sighed, turning towards the entrance of the police station. "Let's get it over with."

Superintendent Cartwright of F Division of the North Yorkshire Police made it clear that he was not amused. From the outset, he insisted on referring to Powell as *Chief* Superintendent, the emphasis a pointed reference to the fact that the rank of chief superintendent had recently been abolished. Not the job, mind you, just the title. Now officers with the rank of superintendent have to apply for the positions previously held by chief superintendents, for which they get extra pay. So, in essence, the rank, duties, and salary of chief superintendent still existed, but the title did not. (Officers, like Powell, who held the rank kept the title.) A classic case of bureaucratic shuffling of the proverbial deck chairs.

Cartwright was a tall man with a thin, humorless face. He indicated that he was willing to cooperate up to a point but basically Powell and Evans were on their own. He ran through the coroner's findings. "A suspicious death, possibly caused by an adder's bite," he concluded.

Powell looked skeptical. "Possibly? What's that supposed to mean?"

"You'd better talk to the pathologist about that," Cartwright said tersely.

Powell noticed that Detective-Sergeant Evans was taking notes. Nothing like initiative. "What about Macfarlane?" he asked.

"What about him?" Cartwright's manner was stiff.

"I understand that he was seen in the neighborhood around the critical time."

"It's all in the file."

"What do you have on him?" Powell persisted.

"Not enough to bring him in," Cartwright admitted. "But he's involved in this, all right."

"What's the name of the officer Macfarlane has brought charges against?"

"Inspector Braughton. He's in charge here."

"I'd like to talk to him."

"He's not involved in the present investigation, for obvious reasons."

"I'd still like to talk to him."

"If you insist."

Cartwright's attitude was beginning to wear a bit thin. "What can you tell me about Dinsdale?" Powell asked.

"What do you want to know?"

Powell was a great one for verbal dueling, but he could hardly be bothered with somebody as predictable as the dull superintendent. "Get on with it, Cartwright," he said wearily.

Cartwright looked at Powell, his eyes narrowing shrewdly. "He was one of the largest landholders in the Moors, a prominent businessman, and a Rotarian, I might add. Very different than that scum, Macfarlane. Now, if there's nothing else, I really must be getting back to Northallerton."

Powell had had about all he could take. "Just so we understand each other, Cartwright," he said evenly, "I like this even less than you do. But if you have a problem, I suggest you talk to the chief constable about it." He got to his feet.

Cartwright shrugged. "I do as I'm told, but we could have handled this one ourselves, no problem." He paused for effect. "After all, we caught *our* Ripper; you're still looking for yours."

"Touché," Sarah Evans remarked, smiling for the first time as they made their way back to the public reception area.

"It's early innings yet," Powell muttered.

Sergeant Evans got the distinct impression that her superior was the type to carry a grudge.

At the desk, Powell signed out the Dinsdale file and inquired about the whereabouts of Inspector Braughton.

"Day off today, sir," the portly sergeant replied cheerily. "Back tomorrow."

"Thank you, Sergeant. I'll pop back then."

"Very good, sir. Cheerio!"

Nothing like the civilized clichés to lubricate the social machinery, Powell thought as they walked out the door. He turned to Sarah Evans. "Why don't we meet in Pickering?" He opened the file folder and riffled through the contents. "I'd like to talk to the pathologist first. Let's see . . . Dr. Alan Harvey. Number Eleven, Birdgate Mews."

"Right."

"By the way," Powell said, "I've booked you into the Lion and Hippo in Brackendale."

"The Lion and Hippo?" she said doubtfully.

Powell smiled. "It's a long story. I'll give you the, er, bare bones over a drink later in the pub."

"The pub."

"Yes, Evans, the pub. Still the wellspring of local information in our increasingly complex and mobile society."

She raised a skeptical eyebrow. "I see."

Powell hopped into his Triumph. "Cheerio."

Powell arrived in Pickering ahead of his colleague. He managed to find a parking spot in the marketplace, lit a cigarette, and waited. The blue dome of heaven above, the imposing Norman tower of the church overlooking the red-roofed houses, and Van the Man on the tape player. He was supposed to be on holiday, but it could be worse, he thought expansively. Despite his earlier reservations, his instincts told him that Sarah Evans was all right. And best of all, at the end of each day—however bright or dreary, bountiful or fruitless—a pint of best Yorkshire bitter awaited him at the Lion and Hippo. He bobbed his head to the beat and drummed on the steering wheel. *I'm a working man in my prime, when I'm cleaning windows—*"

"Sir?" It was Sarah Evans.

"Er, hello, Evans," he said, fumbling with the ignition switch. He scrambled out of the car.

She grinned. "I quite like Van Morrison, sir."

He smiled sheepishly. "Yes, well, it must be nice to have talent."

"I think the street we want is just back there," she said, all businesslike again.

"Right."

They soon located the tidy stone house in a narrow mews near the church. The door and the window trim were painted royal blue. On the side of the step, keeping guard over two empty milk bottles, sat an orange cat. A small brass plaque beside the door discreetly proclaimed A. S. HARVEY, M.D., M.R.C.P., D.P.H. Powell tapped on the door with the polished knocker. A riot of barking erupted in the house followed by the sound of animals hurtling themselves against the door and a raised voice vainly trying to restore order. "Quiet, you mangy lot, quiet!"

Powell and Detective-Sergeant Evans looked at each other. The cat blinked impassively. Eventually the barking stopped and the door opened to reveal a short, balding man with bushy white eyebrows. He held a squirming terrier in each arm and a pack of assorted retrievers and spaniels swarmed around his legs, whining excitedly with tongues lolling. "They haven't had their w-a-l-k today," he explained, spelling the word so as not to incite another orgy of canine frenzy.

Powell introduced Sergeant Evans and himself, explained the purpose of their visit, and apologized for not calling ahead.

"That's quite all right. Please, come in."

Fending off his dogs, Dr. Harvey ushered them down a hallway into a study at the back of the house that had a window looking out on the churchyard. He quickly closed the door behind him. Undeterred, the dogs began to run up and down the hall, slipping and sliding on the hardwood floor. "My wife will be home soon," he said hopefully.

There was a desk beneath the window and on the adjoining walls were tall shelves filled with books. Opposite, against the wall to the right of the door, was a small settee and coffee table. Dr. Harvey gestured towards the settee. "Please," he said.

Powell and Sarah Evans sat down beside each other about as far apart as was physically possible without straddling the arms of the seat. Nonetheless, their legs almost touched.

Dr. Harvey pulled out the chair from his desk, swiveled it around, and sat down himself. "Now then," he said, "what do you want to know?"

"I understand that you conducted the postmortem on Richard Dinsdale," Powell began.

"Yes, an interesting one, that."

"How so?"

"Well, to start with, we don't get many snakebites around these parts. And fatalities are even rarer."

"You're referring to adders, I take it?"

"Right. *Vipera berus*. Quite common on the moors, I'm told, but it's a shy and retiring beast, rarely encountered by people. Dinsdale apparently was one of the unlucky ones."

"He was definitely bitten, then?"

"Unquestionably. There were two puncture marks on the back of his right hand, as would be made by a snake's fangs. In addition, there were external indications of a reaction to the venom—localized inflammation around the puncture wounds, swelling, and so forth. And then of course there was the proverbial smoking gun: one dead male adder found at the scene."

"Dead?"

"Dinsdale's gamekeeper blew its head off."

"Did you attend the scene yourself?"

"No. I was brought in after the fact by the coroner. I'm retired, Chief Superintendent. Used to teach pathology at the University of Leeds. But I still like to keep my hand in."

Powell frowned distractedly. "I'm just wondering how someone could get bitten on the hand? I can see how one might step on a snake . . ."

Harvey shrugged. "Who knows? Strange things happen sometimes. However, you're quite right. The majority of snakebites occur on the foot or lower leg."

"Do you know exactly how it's supposed to have happened?"

Harvey rubbed the top of his head, as if he were trying to stimulate some cranial activity. "Dinsdale was grouse shooting on his estate at the time. A heavy fog set in and the party was up on the moor waiting for conditions to improve. One of Dinsdale's gamekeepers was doing the rounds, checking up on the guns, when he thought he heard a strange sound coming from his employer's shooting butt. By the time he got there, Dinsdale was in pretty rough shape, apparently. The gamekeeper spotted the snake and shot it. That's about it. Dinsdale died a short time later of cardiorespiratory arrest en route to hospital."

"You mentioned before that fatalities in such cases are uncommon. Would you care to elaborate?"

"Adder bites can be potentially fatal for persons with

heart conditions or severe allergies, but such instances are exceedingly rare."

"Did Dinsdale suffer from either of these conditions?"

"There was no indication of cardiac disease. There was, however, some pathology of the lungs, which is suggestive."

"How so?"

"The lungs appeared to be overexpanded and there was some edema present. Microscopic examination of the tissue revealed bronchial abnormalities characteristic of chronic asthma. And as you may know, asthmatics are often prone to various allergies."

"What does the venom actually do to the system?"

"It basically has two modes of action. Firstly, there is a hemorrhagic effect—that is, it causes the red blood cells to break down, which can lead to an impairment of kidney function due to the accumulation of hemoglobin."

Powell noticed with some relief that Sarah Evans was scribbling madly.

"Secondly," Dr. Harvey continued, "the toxin has a depressant action on the central nervous system."

"What are the symptoms?"

"In addition to localized pain and swelling? Nausea and vomiting, disturbed vision, labored breathing. In extreme cases, breathing can stop altogether."

"Do you think Dinsdale's asthma could have been a factor?"

Harvey shrugged. "It's possible."

"You don't sound entirely convinced," Powell observed.

The pathologist looked at Powell. "I'm not," he said, in a careful voice. "And that is why I stated my opinion at the inquest that the cause of death remains unknown."

Powell nodded. "I assume you conducted the usual blood tests?"

"We ran a routine drug screen. His blood alcohol level was high enough to render him intoxicated at the time of his death."

"Is that relevant?"

"Well, alcohol is another depressant, so it could have been a contributing factor but probably not a significant one."

At that moment there was a great commotion of barking and scrabbling feet outside the door, and they heard a woman's voice call out cheerily, "Walkies, babies, walkies!"

"Would you care for a cup of tea?" Dr. Harvey asked hopefully.

Powell smiled and rose from the settee. "Another time, perhaps. I do appreciate your help, Dr. Harvey. If you happen to think of anything else, you can reach us in Brackendale." He handed Harvey one of the business cards he had picked up at the inn.

There was the faint sound of a door slamming and then golden silence. Dr. Harvey sighed. "I'll see you out."

Outside, Sergeant Evans looked disappointed. "I'm dying for a cup of tea," she said.

"Be honest with me, why *did* I get this assignment?" Sarah asked.

Powell sipped his beer. "That," he said, "is a long story. Suffice it to say you have friends in high places."

She looked skeptical. "Really? What about Bill Black? I thought you two always worked together."

"Let's put it this way, Evans: We drew straws and you lost."

She smiled. "Oh, I don't know; I tend to view it as an opportunity."

Powell raised an eyebrow. "Do you now?" He drained his glass and motioned to Robert Walker for another round.

Sarah looked slightly alarmed. "It's getting late, I think perhaps I should turn in—"

"Nonsense, Sergeant, you're in the Murder Squad now. *Dulce est desipere in loco.*"

She regarded him warily. "Pardon?"

Powell smiled innocently. "The evening's just begun—time to relax and reflect on the day's work. It's standard procedure."

"Standard procedure," she repeated doubtfully.

Robert Walker arrived at their table with another pint for Powell and a glass of white wine for Sarah.

When they were alone again, they sat without speaking for a few moments. Then out of the blue she blurted, "Would it be all right if I interviewed the gamekeeper who discovered Dinsdale and the adder?"

Powell regarded her speculatively. Inexperienced, but obviously keen, she exuded an air of competence that he found reassuring. And there was something else about her that he was finding increasingly stimulating as the evening wore on. "Why not?" he said eventually. He reached for his notebook and flipped it open. "I've reviewed the file and made a list of the people we need to talk to." He ran through the list. "Between the two of us, it shouldn't take long to get through it."

Sarah could hardly stop grinning. "Right. I better get started on a list of questions for Mick Curtis. I'll see you at breakfast. Eight-thirty all right?"

Before Powell could protest, Sergeant Evans was making a beeline for the door. Feeling slightly cheated, he caught Walker's eye and ordered another pint.

Putting Sarah Evans out of his mind, he began to analyze his initial impressions of the case. Despite Superintendent Cartwright's glowing description of the late Richard Dinsdale, from what limited information he had been able to pick up in the pub, Powell had come to the conclusion that Dickie hadn't exactly been an endearing character. And the manner of his death was curious at the very least, if not actually suspicious. Fantastic might be a better description. He looked again at his notebook. He decided that he would start by having a word with Katie Elger, supposedly the second person to see Dinsdale immediately before his death. He pulled thoughtfully on his beer.

The next morning in the dining room of the Lion and Hippo, a promising blue sky peeking through chintz curtains boded well for the day ahead. Over breakfast, Powell and Sarah divvied up the names on Powell's list amidst solicitous service from the Walkers (he had to resist the impression that they were trying to eavesdrop). Powell was having the full English, which came complete with a slice of that northern delicacy he tended to regard with a curious mixture of revulsion and relish: black pudding. Sarah, for her part, crunched away with a superior air on a granolalike substance with a Swiss name that sounded like a body secretion. As Mick Curtis lived in Farnmoor and the Elgers up at Dale End Farm, they agreed that it would be best to go their separate ways and meet back at the inn later.

Powell drove the now familiar route to upper Brackendale and took the turning to Dale End Farm. The morning sunlight, filtering through the alders that lined the stream, warmed his face. The leaves were just beginning to take on the bronze hues of autumn, but the fields beside the road were still lush and green. Ahead, the rocky fell that demarcated the head of the dale was dissected by two deep ravines cut by tumbling gills that nourished the infant Merlin, which at this point was no more than a few feet wide. Perched on the high top, overlooking the dale, was the austere facade of Blackamoor Hall.

He pulled up to a large gritstone farmhouse and a young woman emerged from one of the outbuildings, watching him. He waved.

"Ms. Elger?" he called out.

She walked across the muddy farmyard and stood at the gate. Twentyish with frizzy red hair tied loosely at the back and direct blue eyes, she was wearing a University of York sweatshirt. Powell got out of his car.

"Yes?" she said.

Powell introduced himself. "I was wondering if I might have a word. It's about Richard Dinsdale."

She sighed. "You'd better come inside."

Powell followed her to the house, cursing silently as the soft muck oozed up over his shoes. He removed them outside the door.

Katie Elger looked at him with humor in her eyes. "I'll make some tea."

"Splendid."

She ushered him into the large flagstone kitchen and sat him down at the table. Sunlight flooded into the room through a window above the washbasin. She opened the window a little then put the kettle on.

"I understand that you live with your father," Powell began.

"Yes, he's gone into Kirkby. Biscuits?"

"Lovely." He pulled in his stomach and selected a piece of shortbread. "I couldn't help noticing your shirt—are you a student?"

She nodded ruefully. "I was hoping to take a year off to help my father. He's not getting any younger and well, since Mother died, the farm's been a handful for him. But he wouldn't hear of it."

"What are you studying?"

"Biology. I'd like to work here as a park naturalist someday. Milk?"

"Thanks."

She poured the tea.

Powell munched on a chocolate digestive. "What sort of farming do you do?" he asked.

"Hill sheep mostly. We run about fifteen hundred head on two hundred and fifty acres."

"Your father's a tenant farmer, I take it?"

"Serf would be a better word for it," she rejoined angrily.

Powell did not reply, hoping for more unsolicited comment.

"Upland farming is a marginal proposition at best," she explained. "The production of lambs from an upland ewe is about half that from a lowland ewe, as is the gross margin. And that's before you even get started. Then if it's not bracken encroaching into your pastures, it's falling sheep prices. I mean it's hard enough as it is . . ." She seemed about to say something more but apparently thought better of it.

"How long has your father farmed here, Ms. Elger?"

"Over forty years now." A hint of pride in her voice.

"His tenure predates Ronnie Dinsdale taking over Blackamoor, then."

"Old Mr. Dinsdale bought the estate about twenty-five years ago, before I was born. You probably know already that he's the founder of the Dinsdale Supermarket chain . . ."

He nodded. "I understand he's not well."

"He has Alzheimer's, I think. Dickie's been running— I mean, Dickie ran the business for the last few years."

"I've heard that Mr. Dinsdale, senior, is well regarded in the dale."

"According to some folk around these parts, 'e knew knowt aboot farmin' when 'e first come 'ere—but Dad has always spoken well of him."

Powell smiled and sipped his tea. Then his expression turned serious. "I'll come directly to the point, Ms. Elger. I understand that you were one of the last persons to see Dickie Dinsdale alive. I'd like you to tell me exactly what happened."

Katie Elger explained how she had set out from the

shooting box on the day of the farmers' shoot, how she'd gotten lost in the fog, heard the two gunshots, then come across Mick Curtis.

"Tell me exactly what you saw, Ms. Elger."

"It's Katie, please."

"Right. Katie."

"He was just standing there, pointing at Dinsdale, like this." She gestured with her left arm, her eyes wide and staring. "It was freaky. He looked completely shattered, like he'd just seen a ghost or something."

"What did you do then?"

She frowned slightly. "Let's see ... I went over to where he—Dickie—was lying. I remember kneeling down beside him. I thought he might need turning over. He was sort of twitching, and he'd been sick all over himself." She looked at Powell. "It was awful."

"Can you remember anything else about him?"

She thought for a moment. "I think I could smell alcohol."

"Had he been drinking during lunch?"

"Yes, he'd had quite a bit of wine."

"Anything else?"

"Not that I can remember."

"All right, you're beside him in the butt. What happened next?"

She stared at him, her voice hollow. "I saw something moving a few feet away, writhing on the ground ..." She swallowed.

"What was it, Katie?"

She spoke slowly. "A snake—an adder—or what was left of it."

Powell nodded. "What was Mick Curtis doing all this time?"

"Throwing up."

"Tell me, Katie—" He was interrupted by the jangle of the telephone.

She got up and answered it, turning her back to him. "Yes," she murmured. "No, he's gone out. There's someone here. All right." She rang off and returned to the table and sat down.

Powell drained his teacup. "Just one more thing, Katie. I'd like to know what you thought of him—Dickie Dinsdale, I mean."

She met his gaze. "Not much, if you must know."

"Would you care to elaborate?"

Her eyes flashed. "The only thing he cared about was himself. He didn't give a damn about anyone or anything else." She hesitated. "He made it very hard for my father, raising the rent every year. Dale End Farm is my father's whole life—he'd never be happy anywhere else. Don't get me wrong, Mr. Powell. Nobody deserves to die the way Dickie did, but I'm not about to shed any tears for him."

That seemed to be that. "Thanks, Katie. I can let myself out," he added, thinking about his shoes.

As he turned onto the West Daleside Road a few minutes later he saw a red van coming down the road from Blackamoor Rigg. Watching in his rearview mirror, he saw it turn into the road to Dale End Farm.

Emma Walker was worried. She sat in her office looking out the window at the pattern of drystone walls that dissected the landscape like a gargantuan spider web. She held her head in her hands, gently rubbing her temples. She'd felt the unmistakable symptoms of a migraine coming on all morning and there was nothing she could do about it. Nothing she could do about much of anything, come to that. She had started out with the intention of cleaning upstairs but soon realized that she wasn't up to it. She fretted. Now she'd have to hire someone to help with the housekeeping and the meals for a few days. She stared once more at the guest register that lay open on the desk, as if, by simply wishing it, she could erase the last two entries. She sighed and forced herself to move. She needed to talk to Robert while she was still able.

She found him down in the cellar changing over a beer cask. "What are we going to do?" she asked in a monotone.

He stared at her in the gloom. "What are you on about?"

"He's bound to find out about Dad."

Walker went back to his work. "I wouldn't worry about it. He's got nothing to hide, has he? Besides, that's the least of our worries."

She closed her eyes. Her head had begun to throb and she felt unsteady on her feet; she knew that soon the pain would be almost unbearable. She'd be unable to leave her darkened room for days, just when they needed her most. "I'll talk to them," she said quietly.

He turned to watch her as she made her way slowly up the stairs.

CHAPTER 6

Sarah Evans got back to the Lion and Hippo a little after one. Mrs. Walker was nowhere in sight so she went into the pub. Mr. Walker informed her that Mr. Powell had not returned, and would she care for a drink? She checked the time and decided that she might as well grab a bite while she had the chance. She ordered a ploughman's and, after deliberating a moment, a half-pint of Black Sheep best bitter. While Walker was filling her glass, she noticed that there was one other patron. In the corner, an old man in a shapeless cloth cap sat hunched over his pint, staring at her. She smiled at him.

She sat down at a table near the door and, still sensing the eyes of the old man on her, began to pick self-consciously at her lunch. As a distraction, she thought about her interview that morning with Mick Curtis, the gamekeeper—the *head* keeper, as he had made a point of reminding her more than once. She took a sip of her beer. It had gone well enough, she supposed. Curtis's account of the sequence of events leading up to Dinsdale's death had added some useful detail to the description given by Dr. Harvey. It seems that Dinsdale had indeed been drinking heavily on the day in question. They'd gone up on the moor after lunch to wait out the fog. There were apparently eight butts on East Moor where the shoot took place. Dinsdale was in the end butt, the one on the Rosedale side of the moor; the next butt was occupied by Curtis, followed by four farmers (whose names had slipped her mind for the moment), and the young son of one of the farmers. Harry Settle, the former head keeper, was stationed in the last butt, or the one nearest Brackendale. Curtis had mentioned in passing that Settle was no longer employed by the estate, and she got a feeling that there was something going on between them. She made a mental note to follow it up.

She glanced at her drinking companion. The old man was still staring at her. "Lovely afternoon," she remarked loudly.

He grunted something unintelligible and turned his attention to his beer.

Sarah did the same. According to Curtis, fog is an occupational hazard for a gamekeeper. The weather up on the moors can change from one minute to the next, so the usual policy is to sit tight and wait for the fog to lift long enough so you can finish the drive. She imagined that being able to see what you're shooting at would be a bonus. On the day of the farmers' shoot, however, the fog had proven to be thick and persistent. Once settled, the party waited in their shooting butts for about half an hour. As the mist was showing no signs of abating, Curtis had decided to make the rounds to canvas his companions, including Dinsdale.

As Curtis had approached his employer, he could hear agonized groans. He had rushed over and found Dinsdale lying on the ground. As he was about to see what he could do for him, he saw the adder. He told her it was a bit of a blur after that; he remembered shooting the snake, seeing Katie Elger and the others, and then being sick. Sarah shivered. She'd have fainted on the spot! Like Curtis, she had a thing about snakes.

The phone in the office began to ring and Robert Walker left the bar to answer it. Sarah finished her beer, got up, and walked over to the old man's table. "I was wondering if you could help me," she said brightly.

The man looked at her with bloodshot eyes. "Oh, aye?" he rumbled.

"I'm looking for Harry Settle, the gamekeeper. Do you know where I might find him?"

"Aye." Silence.

"Where does he live, then?"

"Ah knows who tha' is, lass," the old man said archly.

Sarah groaned inwardly. "Oh, yes?"

"Past t' garage about a half mile, down by t' beck."

Was she imagining it, or had he lowered his voice slightly in a conspiratorial manner? Everyone wants to be a cop, she thought. She thanked him, and as she walked out of the bar she decided that she'd better head up to her room to do up her notes before she forgot something important.

The next thing she knew, there was an annoyingly persistent banging in her head. She opened her eyes, unsure for a moment where she was. She was lying on her bed, fully clothed, a molten flood of afternoon sunlight pouring through the bay window. Someone was pounding on the door. She held her watch in front of her face and blinked blearily. "Good God!" She leapt to her feet and stumbled towards the door. She fumbled with the lock, eventually managing to wrestle the door open.

A smiling Powell, formulating the witty remark.

"Don't say anything," she warned.

"I've come to invite you to dinner," he replied innocently. "And I must say you look smashing."

She grimaced. "I'll be down in twenty minutes." She shut the door in his face.

The harried-looking landlord was clearing away the traces of the grilled salmon and buttered courgettes from their table. Powell and Sarah Evans were the only customers in the dining room, but Walker had his hands full serving them as well as his patrons in the pub next door. "Missus is under the weather," he explained hurriedly. "Give me a shout if you need anything else," he said, as he dashed back into the bar.

Powell raised his glass. "Here's to success."

"I'll drink to that," Sarah replied, taking a sip of her wine. Then she leaned back in her chair and sighed contentedly. "That was bloody marvelous."

"Standard procedure, Sergeant. The detection of crime is a sport of noble minds, and to function at peak efficiency one must properly nourish the little gray cells."

She smiled crookedly. "If I drink any more wine, I won't have any little gray cells."

"We'd better get down to work, then," Powell rejoined. "I've been meaning to ask you how you got on with Curtis."

With an admirable attention to detail, Sarah recounted the gist of her conversation with the gamekeeper. "Whatever happened must have happened during the thirty minutes or so that Dinsdale was alone in his butt waiting for the fog to lift," she concluded. "By the time Curtis got to him he was already in a bad state, so I should think that he may have been bitten sooner rather than later. To know for certain, we'd need to know how long the venom takes to act."

This seemed to arouse Powell's interest. "And Curtis didn't hear anything suspicious during this time?"

Sarah shrugged. "Apparently not. But then he was some distance away. As I understand it, the butts are about forty yards apart. Curtis says he didn't hear a thing from Dinsdale until he went over to check up on him."

Powell grunted. "It seems to fit. When Katie Elger— that's Frank Elger's daughter—showed up on the scene, she found Curtis as white as a sheet, standing over Dinsdale, who was probably beyond hope by then." He frowned slightly. "Wouldn't you think, though, that someone who had just been bitten by a venomous snake would cry out or call for help?"

"He was drunk, wasn't he?" Sarah observed.

"True." Powell emptied his glass. "What was your general impression of Curtis?"

Sarah thought about this for a moment. "Rather fancies himself, I'd say. He spoke highly of Dinsdale, and I gathered that the feeling was mutual. Dinsdale recently promoted him to head keeper, apparently. I got the feeling, though, that there was something going on between Curtis and the former head keeper, Harry Settle."

"Really? It wouldn't hurt to follow that up."

She nodded. "Tomorrow I'd like to drive over to Helmsley," she said. "The National Park headquarters are located there. I thought it might be a good idea to bone up on adders."

"I didn't think you liked snakes."

"There's all sorts of things I don't like that I have to put up with," she said pointedly.

Powell ignored this. "While you're brushing up on your herpetology, I'll pay a visit to Blackamoor Hall. It's about time I introduced myself."

Sarah stared at the fire roaring in the hearth. She suddenly felt very warm and the atmosphere seemed stifling.

"Why don't we get some fresh air?" Powell was saying.

"What? Oh, yes—I'd like that," she said.

The sun dipped behind the dark curve of the hill as they walked together beside the beck, the sounds of the village—a woman calling to her child, a barking dog, and the shouts of small boys playing football on the green— were submerged in the murmur of rushing water.

Sarah breathed deeply. "I've often thought it would be lovely to live in a place like this," she said.

Powell grunted in a noncommittal fashion. "Tell me, Sarah—by the way, may I call you Sarah?"

"What am I supposed to call you, then? Sir? Mr. Powell?"

He shrugged. "Erskine, or just Powell if you prefer."

She looked skeptical. "It's a bit informal, isn't it? Suppose I forget myself back at the Yard? I'd be drummed out."

"Well, we're in the field now. Things are always a bit informal in the field."

She smiled in spite of herself. "I know, standard procedure. You were going to ask me something just then."

"I was wondering what Merriman sees in you," Powell said mischievously.

A puzzled expression on her face. "What do you mean?"

"Apparently he has plans for you."

She colored. "You must be joking!"

Powell described the circumstances in which Merriman had assigned her to the case.

"Good God! I hope you don't think . . ." She was suddenly angry. "I don't need him or anyone else to pull strings for me. I'll succeed on my own merit or not at all—I refuse to be a bloody statistic in one of his self-serving PC schemes."

"An admirable sentiment, but I wouldn't look a gift horse in the mouth, if I were you. You could be back in the office pushing paper right now."

She sighed. "There is that. But what about you?"

"What about me?"

"I mean, how do you cope?" She searched in vain for the right words. "You know . . . with the Merrimans of the world."

He hesitated for a moment. "It's the job—this damnable job. It keeps me going, keeps me thinking. Or keeps me *from* thinking. I don't know." He smiled thinly. "In the grander scheme of things, Merriman and his ilk are the least of my worries."

She was taken aback by such an unexpected display of candor from her superior and was unable to think of a reply. They walked along for a while without speaking. The wind began to pipe up and Sarah shivered. "It's getting late," she said. "We should be getting back."

"Yes, of course," Powell said, trying to conceal his disappointment.

It seemed that in no time at all they were back at the inn. They stood at the bottom of the stairs for an awkward moment.

"Well, until tomorrow, then," he said.

She smiled. "Good night."

Powell retired to the pub to contemplate a time long ago when lions roared in the forests of Yorkshire and hippos basked in the warm waters of Ryedale.

CHAPTER 7

Blackamoor Hall was a sprawling pile of dark gritstone with a Tudor wing added on, a riot of complicated roof angles, and an impressive number of jutting chimneys (which had something to do, one assumed, with the long and bleak moorland winter). Built in the seventeenth century on the site of a twelfth-century nunnery (the irony of which would soon become evident), the house was situated on what was known as West Moor, high above upper Brackendale and west of the Blackamoor Rigg Road. It is said that the nuns of neighboring Rosedale Abbey used to make the pilgrimage to the nunnery at Blackamoor to contemplate the deeper realities. Interestingly, the austere and purifying landscape upon which they came to meditate was a creation of the monastic movement itself, a sort of spiritual application of Heisenberg's uncertainty principle. For the North York Moors, now considered one of Britain's beauty spots, is in reality a devastated wasteland, despoiled by the same hands that built the first and greatest of the Cistercian abbeys at Rievaulx.

Starting with the first modest efforts of Bronze Age hunters who began clearing the forests to make hunting easier, followed by Iron Age craftsmen who needed wood to stoke their primitive blast furnaces, the process of deforestation was greatly accelerated by the monks of Rievaulx Abbey who cleared the valleys for cultivation and turned vast herds of sheep loose on the uplands. The great forests were eventually replaced by grass, heather, and bracken—the only plants capable of growing on the impoverished, acidified soils. Nowadays the moors are actively maintained in this condition by a few wealthy landowners for the benefit of sheep and grouse.

Powell had learned from Robert Walker that the Blackamoor estate comprised some forty-five hundred acres, which included upper Brackendale, most of the village, and two thousand acres of grouse moors. There were a dozen or so tenant farmers like Frank Elger, each farming two hundred or so acres in the dale and grazing their sheep on common moorland. He got the impression from Katie Elger that the position of the tenant farmers was a bit dodgy, depending as it did on general economic conditions as well as the inclinations of the landlord.

Dickie Dinsdale had, according to Walker, run the estate into the ground through mismanagement, while at the same time raising the rents of his tenants to the point, if one believed Katie, where good farmers were finding it difficult to survive. Hardly a recipe for social harmony. Then Dinsdale turns up dead under circumstances that could be considered highly unusual, to say the least.

Such were Powell's thoughts as he mounted the broad stone steps of Blackamoor Hall. The black-haired woman who answered the door could have been any age from thirty to forty. She had a cadaverous complexion with dark, nervous eyes and spoke with a Spanish accent.

"Mrs. Dinsdale is expecting me," Powell said.

The woman averted her eyes. "Yes, sir. Please come this way."

Powell followed her from the entrance hall, through a large high-ceilinged and oddly shabby-looking room—which he guessed had served as a ballroom in better days, complete with spiral staircase—then down a long passage leading to the Tudor wing.

The woman stopped at a door on the left side of the corridor, knocking lightly before opening it. "Chief Superintendent Powell, madam," she announced.

Another woman's voice answered, "Thank you, Francesca."

As Powell entered the room—either a large study or a small library—a razor-thin woman with a bouffant hairstyle rose from her writing table to greet him. Behind her, a large window provided a splendid view of the dale below. She extended her hand and smiled pleasantly. "Welcome to Blackamoor Hall, Chief Superintendent. I'm Marjorie Dinsdale." A trace of an accent indicated that she was no stranger to the sound of London's Bow bells.

Powell took a seat across the table from his host. Immaculately coiffed and made-up—quite striking in an ostentatious sort of way—Marjorie Dinsdale looked to be in her late fifties and obviously spent a considerable amount of time and effort on her appearance. "Thank you for agreeing to see me on such short notice, Ms. Dinsdale," he began. "I wish to offer my condolences. I know this must be a difficult time for you—"

"It's *Mrs.*," she interrupted. "I'm not one for political correctness, Mr. Powell."

Powell smiled fleetingly. "One has to tread carefully these days, Mrs. Dinsdale," he said. "I'll try to make this as brief as possible. As I explained on the telephone, due to the unusual nature of your son's accident, I've been sent up from London to assist the local police with their inquiry into the matter."

She raised a skeptical eyebrow. "You mean, you think that Dickie's death was not an accident?"

"At this point I'm trying to keep an open mind. On the face of it, there is no reason to think that **it** was anything other than a freak mishap."

"I see. You should know for starters, Mr. Powell, that Dickie was not my son."

"Oh?"

"He was my stepson. I'm Ronnie's—that's his father— second wife. We were married in nineteen-eighty-nine. Dickie was twenty-six at the time."

"Do you have any children of your own, Mrs. Dinsdale?"

"A daughter, Felicity."

"I understand, Mrs. Dinsdale, that your husband is not well . . ."

Mrs. Dinsdale looked out the window as if searching for something amidst the green sheep-dotted pastures.

"He's very frail, very forgetful—he doesn't even know who I am most of the time."

"I'm sorry."

She sighed. "He's worked so hard all his life. To end up like this . . ."

Time to test the waters. "I'd like you to tell me about Dickie, Mrs. Dinsdale."

She looked at him with an odd expression on her face. "What do you want to know?"

"For starters, did he take an active part in the running of the Dinsdale business empire?"

Mrs. Dinsdale frowned. "Empire? Dinsdale's is a family business, Chief Superintendent, not some sort of faceless conglomerate. Ronnie started out as a green-grocer with a corner store in Leeds, and he built up his business through sheer bloody determination and hard work. Dinsdale's was at one time the largest independent supermarket chain in the north of England," she said, a note of pride resonating in her voice.

"You said *was*."

She appraised him cooly. "You're very observant, Chief Superintendent. Poor Dickie didn't have much of a head for business. When Ronnie was no longer able to manage, Dickie took over and, well, the last few years have been rather difficult."

Was there a hint of bitterness in her voice? "What about the day-to-day running of the estate? Did Dickie take care of that as well?"

"Yes." Her terseness spoke volumes.

"I don't mean to pry, Mrs. Dinsdale, but I've been wondering about the mechanics of running a large estate these days . . ."

She sighed. "It's a constant struggle. You have to maintain and modernize—keep up with the times, as Ronnie used to say. And most of all, it takes money."

"I imagine the shooting brings in some revenue," Powell ventured.

"Yes, if it's properly managed," she said pointedly.

It seemed like old Dickie was a right cockup. Changing gears, Powell said, "On the day of the accident, I understand that your stepson was participating in an annual event known as the farmers' shoot. I'd be grateful if you could tell something about it."

"It was something Ronnie initiated soon after taking over Blackamoor. As you may know, the helpers on a grouse shoot—the beaters and so on—are recruited by the head keeper from the ranks of the local farmers and farmworkers. For their trouble, they get a day off from the normal routine, lunch, a bottle of beer or two, and a few quid. However, Ronnie felt that they deserved special recognition for their contribution, so once a year he provided them with a day of shooting." She smiled faintly. "Ronnie used to pitch in as a beater on these occasions, and I think he enjoyed himself as much as his tenants did."

"I take it his son carried on the tradition."

"Yes." Once again her customary loquaciousness in relation to her husband was reduced to terse, monosyllabic responses when she was asked about her late stepson.

"I understand that Dickie recently promoted Mick Curtis to the position of head keeper," Powell continued. "I'm wondering about the former head keeper—Harry Settle. Did he retire?"

Mrs. Dinsdale hesitated. "There was an incident this August. Dickie blamed Harry for it."

"You're referring, I take it, to the protest organized by Stumpy Macfarlane?"

She nodded.

"Did Dickie actually sack Settle, then?"

"Demoted, I think, would be a better word for it."

"What do you mean?"

Mrs. Dinsdale sighed. "Dickie offered him Mick Curtis's old job of underkeeper. Not surprisingly, he decided to retire instead."

"When did this take effect?"

"The last day of August."

"But I understand that Settle participated in the farmers' shoot some two weeks later."

"Harry organized the event for years. I think he felt he owed it to the others—it was sort of his swan song, you might say."

"Did you have an opinion about your stepson's decision to replace Settle?"

"I didn't agree with it, actually. I like Harry. He was gamekeeper here when my husband took over the estate, and Ronnie thought the world of him. However, Dickie made all the day-to-day decisions."

"What can you tell me about Mick Curtis, Mrs. Dinsdale?"

"Harry hired him about five years ago." She did not offer to elaborate.

Something was bothering Powell. "Tell me, Mrs. Dinsdale, how does Blackamoor rank in the scheme of things, as far as grouse shoots go, I mean?"

She considered this for a moment. "In terms of the annual bag, smallish, I'd say."

He looked puzzled. "I wonder why Stumpy would pick Blackamoor to stage a protest? His protests are usually related to environmental issues—why would he turn his attention to the anti–blood sport cause?"

She eyed him shrewdly. "That would depend on what his point was, wouldn't it, Chief Superintendent?"

Powell persisted. "Mrs. Dinsdale, can you think of any reason why a well-known environmental activist like Stumpy would target a grouse shoot at Blackamoor? Could there be something related to the family's other business interests, perhaps?"

"I can assure you that Dinsdale's sells only dolphin-friendly tinned tuna, Chief Superintendent," she said stiffly.

"I see." His expression turned solemn. "You're aware that deaths from adder bites are extremely rare, Mrs. Dinsdale?"

"Yes." Wary now.

"I understand that your stepson suffered from asthma."

She nodded, a glimmer of hope in her eyes. "Oh, yes, he had terrible allergies."

"Perhaps that explains it," Powell said carefully.

"Yes, I imagine it does," she said.

Powell got to his feet. "I won't take up any more of your time, Mrs. Dinsdale. It was very kind of you to see me on such short notice. I'll be in touch if anything comes up."

"Thank you, Chief Superintendent," she said vaguely. "Francesca will see you out."

Standing at the door was the black-haired, dark-eyed servant, who had miraculously appeared right on cue.

As Powell drove back down to Brackendale, reflecting on his interview with Marjorie Dinsdale, he could not suppress the feeling that things were not quite as they seemed at Blackamoor Hall.

Marjorie Dinsdale picked up the telephone and pressed the numbers mechanically. "Inspector Braughton, please."

After a few seconds, a voice on the other end. "Braughton."

"It's Marjorie."

A pause. "How did it go?"

"He asked a lot of questions."

"What sort of questions?"

"What do you think?" she said acidly. "You're a policeman."

"Why did you call, Marjorie?" he asked, his manner stiff now.

"Can't you do something about it? I'm concerned about the publicity—you know it would kill Ronnie."

Braughton resisted the temptation to point out that old Ronnie couldn't tell his arse from a tea kettle in his present state. "Look, Marjorie, you must understand I've got to keep my head down. I'll try to keep you abreast. That's all I can do. I'm sorry. Now I must go."

"Jim, I—" *Click.*

She sat staring out the window for a considerable length of time. She wondered what Ronnie would've done in similar circumstances. She rang for Francesca.

"Francesca, have you seen Miss Felicity?"

Francesca averted her eyes. "No, madam."

Mrs. Dinsdale sighed. "Have Luis bring the car around."

"Yes, madam."

Mrs. Dinsdale returned her attention to the bleak and windswept prospect beyond her window. Low clouds now shrouded the monochrome tops and she could feel the vibration of the wind against the glass. Her sharp features tightened into a frown. What had seemed so simple was now getting complicated.

CHAPTER 8

That evening, Powell and Detective-Sergeant Evans sat in the Lion and Hippo comparing notes. The atmosphere in the pub seemed perfectly normal—the general hum of conversation, a boisterous game of darts in the corner, a young couple mooning over each other in the snug—the sort of scene that was no doubt being played out at that very moment in a thousand other pubs around the country. But for Powell, the mood that prevailed in the Lion and Hippo struck a slightly dissonant note. Here was a group of people whose village, farms, and homes were owned lock, stock, and barrel by a mental incompetent whose only son and heir had just died in the most bizarre and horrible fashion, yet you'd never know it by looking at them. He mentioned it to Sarah.

She shrugged. "Life goes on, I guess."

"Thanks for pointing that out," he rejoined dryly. "Still," he added on a more sober note, "I imagine that the future of the estate—and by extension, the future of all of Brackendale—must be a bit up in the air. Which reminds me, we need to check the probate registry for the details of Dickie Dinsdale's will. I'd be interested to learn who benefits from his death."

"Right."

"How did you make out in Helmsley, by the way?"

"I spoke to one of the National Park ecologists," she said eagerly. "She gave me bags of literature about adders, if you'd care to read . . ."

"I'm afraid I'm not one for bedtime reading. Why don't you distill it for me?"

Sarah summarized what she had learned about the natural history of adders, the only poisonous snake indigenous to the British Isles. Growing to a length of about two feet, adders are fairly common in the North York Moors Park, but, due to a secretive nature, they are rarely seen by the casual observer. As Dr. Harvey had indicated, their bite is not usually serious, although fatalities have been known to occur in cases where the victim experienced a severe allergic reaction or suffered from a heart condition. Adders tend to live a solitary life in the spring and summer but congregate in the autumn in abandoned animal dens and the like where they come together in a writhing mass—Sarah was unable to suppress a shudder at this point—primarily to retain heat during the winter months, it's thought, but possibly also for reproductive reasons. "A sort of snake sex orgy," she commented.

Powell smiled. "Fascinating. I wonder how they'd sort each other out."

She ignored him and continued. "Interestingly, adders

are also known to frequent cavities in drystone walls at this time of year."

This caught Powell's attention. "What about shooting butts?"

She shrugged. "I don't see why not."

"I wonder how difficult it would be to capture one?" Powell mused.

"I asked her about that. She said she once caught one using a butterfly net."

"Do you like Indian food, by the way?" he asked casually.

"Pardon?" She looked slightly bewildered.

He looked at her. "You know, curry."

"I love curry, but what does that have to do with . . . ?"

"I've prevailed upon our landlord to let me take over the kitchen later this evening. I thought I'd, er, make us dinner. I mean, if it's not too late . . ."

She smiled mischievously, amused by her superior's awkwardness. "I don't mind waiting, if it's worth waiting for."

Powell signaled to Robert Walker for another round. "On the surface of it," he said after he'd returned to their table with another pint of Tetley's for himself and a shandy for her, "the whole thing seems plausible enough—yet somehow it just doesn't *feel* right."

An interesting choice of words, Sarah thought. "I know exactly what you mean," she agreed. "Too neat and tidy." She sipped her drink and considered her superior with renewed interest. Forty-something, she guessed, and handsome in a reserved sort of way. She had known him previously only by reputation; amongst the Met rank and file, he had street cred, which counted for something. Although she had bumped into him a few times at the Yard, he'd barely acknowledged her. He didn't give the impression of being a snob, exactly—preoccupied might be a better word for it. During their short time working together, however, she'd found him to be an agreeable, if slightly self-conscious companion. And best of all, he'd given her free rein to follow her nose.

"I talked to Dr. Harvey again this afternoon," Powell was saying. "A severe asthma attack could conceivably lead to death within thirty minutes. But despite the fact that Dinsdale had one of those puffer things on him, there was no trace of the drug in his system."

She frowned slightly. "But even if he didn't have an actual attack, his asthma might have made him more sensitive to the snake's venom, right?"

He nodded. "Right." His eyes tripped lightly over her. She was twenty years younger than he was and pleasant to look at. Keen, ambitious, and, from what he'd seen of her so far, highly capable. "Who's next on our contact list?" he asked.

"How about I do the ex–head keeper, Harry Settle?"

Powell nodded. "And I think I'll have a little chat with Inspector Braughton."

"You don't think there's anything to Stumpy's charge of police brutality, do you?"

Powell shrugged. "It happens."

She tossed him a strange look. "In my experience, people who break the law tend to be the authors of their own misfortune."

"Perhaps. But, in *my* experience, it's generally best to

leave matters of retribution to the courts, God, or the wheel of karma—take your pick."

She colored. "Of course, sir, I didn't mean ..." She trailed off lamely.

Powell smiled to put her at ease. "I'll try to get to the bottom of it when I talk to Braughton. I need to know where we stand when I eventually talk to old Stumpy." He emptied his glass with a prodigious gulp. "Now, then, it's time to start dinner. Roll up your sleeves, woman."

She looked wary. "I thought you were making *me* dinner."

He laughed. "Nonsense! It's never any fun just watching. You're going to have a hands-on experience, as they say. Now drink up."

Powell bustled purposefully about the spacious kitchen of the Lion and Hippo. "Right, we're almost ready," he said cheerily. "Chop the garlic and ginger as finely as you can."

A mock salute from Sergeant Evans. "Aye, aye, sir!"

"It's bloody marvelous being able to work in a kitchen like this," he added as an aside, surveying the gleaming gas cooker and the assortment of copper saucepans hanging from the old beams.

"Here you are," said Sarah. "One tablespoon fresh garlic, two tablespoons ginger root, finely chopped."

"Now, I want you to pay close attention; I'm only going to do this once." He gestured towards a cast-iron pot sitting on the flaming cooker. "I'm heating a quarter cup of cooking oil on high heat. By rights, I should be using a *karai*, which is a sort of Indian wok, but any heavy pot will do. Before we get started, I'll run through the ingredients."

These were arrayed on a large butcher's block beside the range. He pointed to each item in turn: "Garlic and ginger; one pound of fresh leg of lamb, cut into one-inch cubes; one medium onion, sliced; a green bell pepper, chopped into one-inch pieces; a small tomato, coarsely chopped; half a cup of canned crushed tomatoes; half a teaspoon of ground red chilies, more if you like—"

"I like it hot," she interjected.

He raised an eyebrow. "All right, one teaspoon of chili powder. A teaspoon of paprika and half a teaspoon or so of salt."

Sarah had produced her notebook and was scribbling madly.

"Before I begin, I should point out that the *karai* style of cooking originated in northwest Pakistan and—"

"Could you get on with it?" Sarah prompted. "I'm bloody famished."

"Right. We start off with our garlic and ginger—" a loud sizzle as the ingredients hit the hot oil "—and stir-fry for about thirty seconds. Now we add everything else except the green pepper and fresh tomato. The trick is to keep stirring and shaking the pot like this so that nothing will stick." A rhythmic clattering as Powell worked both hands. "This should take about twenty minutes. I'll add the green pepper and fresh tomato near the end." An intoxicating aroma began to fill the kitchen. Bloody marvelous, Sarah thought. He cooks, too . . .

While Powell presided over the *karai* lamb, Sarah busied herself with the rice.

"Voilà!" Powell announced, setting the fragrant pot on a small table set in the corner of the kitchen.

Sarah nearly muscled him aside, trying to get her nose over the pot. She sniffed ecstatically. Tender morsels of lamb glazed with spices and tomato amidst a garnish of green pepper.

"You won't be served until you sit down," Powell said sternly.

She didn't argue.

Half an hour later, Sarah stuck out her tongue and began to fan it with her hand. Then she leaned back and sighed contentedly. "Can we do that again some time?" she asked.

"I always like to smoke afterward," he said, feeling for his cigarettes.

She smiled tolerantly. "Where did you learn to cook like that?"

"From a master. Do you know the K2 Tandoori in Charlotte Street?"

She shook her head.

"The proprietor, Rashid Jamal, is an old friend of mine. The K2 is a fertile oasis in my otherwise arid existence."

She smiled and took a sip of her lager. "You don't seem like the arid type to me."

"You'd be surprised."

"I'd like to try it some time."

"Hmm?" He exhaled a cloud of smoke.

"The K2."

"I'll take you there for lunch when we get back."

"I'd like that. My older brother and his mates used to occasionally drag me along on their university pub crawls.

We always ended up in some curry house about three in the morning."

"You'll make some lager lout a fine wife," Powell observed dryly.

"Not a chance. I'm going to be commissioner some day," Sarah asserted, only half jokingly.

Powell grimaced as he pushed himself away from the table. "I can see that you need to be taught some humility. I'll wash, you dry."

The next day dawned dreary and wet. Brackendale was shrouded in low clouds that obscured the high tops, creating an oppressive, slightly claustrophobic atmosphere. Powell was more than happy to escape to Malton to see Inspector Braughton and leave Sarah Evans behind to pursue the locals. He had called the previous afternoon to set up an appointment with Braughton, who had not exactly been enthusiastic about the prospect of a meeting. Powell was certain, however, that the local inspector would be able to provide some useful information.

As he pulled off the A169 onto the Old Malton Road, the drizzle turned into a downpour, drumming a fierce tattoo on the roadster's convertible top. Rather alarmingly, water had begun to drip onto the passenger seat. A few minutes later, he pulled into the car park at the police station and parked as close to the entrance as he could. He removed the ashtray from the dash, opened his door a crack and dumped the contents outside. Filthy habit, he thought. He carefully placed the ashtray on the seat beside him to catch the drips. Then he bailed out of the car and made a run for it.

An hour later, Powell was still sitting in Inspector Braughton's office.

"After Dinsdale hit him, then what?" he asked in an even voice.

Braughton hesitated. "I cautioned Macfarlane and was about to take him into custody when Dickie—I mean Mr. Dinsdale—pointed his shotgun at the lad—" he swallowed "—then he pulled the trigger."

Powell stared at Braughton in disbelief. "He did *what*?"

"The gun w-was unloaded, of course," Braughton stammered, as if this excused everything. "Look, I know it doesn't look good. If I had it to do over again, I'd have done something about it, but it's water under the bridge now, isn't it?"

"Christ Almighty, Braughton. Leaving aside your duty as a policeman for a moment, didn't it occur to you that Stumpy would crucify you in the media over this? And who could blame him?"

Braughton said nothing.

"And bad press is the least of your worries. I hear you've also been charged with assault."

"It'll be my word against Macfarlane's, won't it?"

"You'll be testifying under oath," Powell reminded him.

Braughton averted his eyes. "When we arrived on the scene, an unlawful protest was in progress," he said in a practiced monotone. "Emotions were running high and there may well have been some rough stuff before we were able to intervene and restore order. It's as simple as that." He ran his hand over the top of his balding head in a nervous gesture and seemed slightly surprised to find little but skin.

"Who tipped you off to Stumpy's plans?"

"Mr. Dinsdale."

Powell's expression evinced surprise.

"A few days before the Twelfth," Braughton explained, "he called to say that he had reason to believe that Macfarlane was planning to disrupt the shoot. After the trouble on Ilkey Moor last year, we took the threat seriously. We arranged to wait at the Hall while the shoot was in progress, then move in when we got the call from one of the gamekeepers."

"Mick Curtis?"

Braughton nodded.

"Did Dinsdale provide any evidence to support his claim that he'd been targeted by Stumpy?"

"Evidence? He turned out to be bloody right, didn't he?" Braughton said indignantly.

"Let's cut to the chase, shall we, Braughton? I understand that Stumpy was seen in the neighborhood around the time of Dinsdale's death. I get the impression that Superintendent Cartwright suspects foul play and considers Stumpy the prime suspect."

Braughton looked uncomfortable. "Macfarlane was stopped the day before by a constable in a routine check on Blackamoor Rigg Road, literally in sight of the Hall."

"A routine check," Powell repeated, a skeptical note in his voice.

"Aye, as it so happens."

"Go on."

"When the constable checked his driver's licence and realized who it was, he asked him what he was doing in the vicinity of Blackamoor Hall." He paused before delivering the punch line. "Sightseeing was what he said."

"Where does he live?"

"York. He's a student at the university."

"I'll need his address. By the way, has anyone talked to him since Dinsdale's death?"

Braughton nodded sourly. "He's got an alibi of sorts. His girlfriend claims he was with her. Chloe Aldershot, her name is. Another bloody student. She's one of the protesters charged along with Macfarlane, so I'd take her word with a grain of salt. Daughter of Lord Aldershot and a flaming anarchist, that one."

Powell frowned. "I'll need her address and telephone number, as well." There was something gnawing away at the back of his brain, but he couldn't quite grab a hold of it. "Did you know Dinsdale, on a personal basis, I mean?"

Braughton shrugged. "I met him on a few occasions through his stepmother. Mrs. Dinsdale and I are both members of the local horticultural society. We share a passion for orchids."

"What was your impression of him?"

Braughton seemed to consider the question carefully before replying. "He had an abrasive nature, you'd have to say. Bit of a know-it-all. He gave the impression that he enjoyed the trappings of wealth—the shooting and so on—but didn't like to get his hands dirty."

"What about Mrs. Dinsdale?"

"The exact opposite. Although she's originally from London, she fit right into the country life: secretary of the local hunt club, keen gardener and birder—that sort of thing. Much like her husband."

"You seem to know her quite well," Powell observed.

Braughton rubbed his hand over the top of his head. "Not really."

"Can you think of anyone who might have had it in for him?"

"You're asking the wrong person."

Powell scrutinized Braughton closely. "What do you think happened to him?"

"I think a snake killed him," the inspector said slowly. "End of story."

CHAPTER 9

Sarah Evans eventually located the gamekeeper's cottage about half a mile north of the village. At the point where the road turned sharply east to cross over the River Merlin, a rough road, made muddy from the recent rain, took off to the left towards a cluster of buildings set on the bank of the river. A small faded sign affixed to the corner of the stone wall at the turning simply stated ROSE COTTAGE. As Sarah's car lurched along the track, the wheels churning and slipping through the miniature lakes that had formed in the potholes, she had visions of getting stuck and having to get pulled out. Not an auspicious start to an official visit.

She eventually made it, however, and pulled up in front of the house, a tidy stone cottage with a large garden in front that would have looked bright and cheerful on a good day, she didn't doubt, but today looked rather forlorn and dreary. A black Labrador retriever sat on the step watching her. Behind the cottage was a series of long, low pens constructed of posts and wire mesh, containing hundreds of colorful cock pheasants. The birds milled about and clucked nervously as Sarah got out of her car. The dog began to bark halfheartedly.

As she walked up to the door of the cottage, she marveled at the bewildering variety of outbuildings, as well as the various bits of machinery, equipment, and containers scattered around the yard, the functions of which were a complete mystery to her. She was a city girl through and through and didn't mind admitting it. She cautiously held her hand out to the dog who snuffled at her with its grizzled muzzle.

An older woman opened the door. Sarah introduced herself and explained the purpose of her visit.

"You'd better come in, dear, or you'll catch your death," Mrs. Settle said.

She escorted Sarah into a small sitting room overlooking the river. The room was rather starkly furnished with a settee, a matching wing chair, and a small coffee table. It was strangely devoid of the normal bric-a-brac and mementos one would have expected an older couple to have accumulated over the years. A number of cardboard boxes sat on the floor.

"Please forgive the mess, Miss Evans. The moving van will be here next week," Mrs. Settle said by way of explanation. "You 'ave a seat and I'll get us a nice cup of tea."

Sarah smiled. "I'd like nothing better, Mrs. Settle." After her hostess left the room, Sarah had a look around. She glanced into one of the open boxes and was surprised to see a photo of a smiling Mr. and Mrs. Walker amongst the other knickknacks. She sat down in the chair and turned to look out the window. Across the river she could make out some red-roofed farm buildings, indistinct in the mist. Dale End Farm? she wondered abstractedly. She knew she should remain emotionally detached, but she felt sorry for the Settles. Mr. Settle losing his job and being forced to leave his home after all these years, because of a silly protest that had been beyond the former gamekeeper's power to prevent. And with Dinsdale dead, the whole thing now seemed so unnecessary. But the die had been cast, she supposed, and—

Her thoughts were interrupted by the return of Mrs. Settle who was accompanied by a heavyset, stolid-looking man with thinning gray hair.

"Now, don't get up, dear," Mrs. Settle admonished. "This is my husband, Harry. Harry, I'd like you to meet Sergeant Evans. She's a detective from Scotland Yard," she added significantly.

Sarah smiled and exchanged greetings with Mr. Settle. She attempted to make small talk as Mrs. Settle arranged the tea things and a plate of homemade shortbread on the coffee table. When everything was to her liking, Mrs. Settle nestled on the settee beside her husband.

Sarah was wondering how to handle the potentially delicate subject of the Settles' present situation during the interview. Best to get it over with and clear the air, she decided. She took out her notebook and brushed a strand of hair from her forehead. "Mr. Settle, I understand that you were head keeper at Blackamoor until recently."

Settle's expression darkened. "That's so."

"I'd like to ask you some questions about what happened on September thirteenth of this year, the day of the farmers' shoot."

"Oh, aye?" he rumbled.

"I understand that you were present on East Moor that day."

He grunted in what she took as the affirmative. Mr. Settle was clearly a man of few words.

"Were you still employed by the estate at that time?"

"Nay."

"When did you leave the employ of the estate, Mr. Settle?"

"End of August."

"Would you mind telling me why you left?"

"I bloody quit," Settle said with uncharacteristic emotion in his voice.

Sarah drew a mental breath. "Why did you quit, Mr. Settle?"

With obvious reluctance, he recounted what had happened on August twelfth: the protest by the group of antis, how Dickie Dinsdale had blamed him for it and then humiliated him by giving his job to his former assistant, Mick Curtis.

"It was worse than sackin' 'im outright," Mrs. Settle piped in. "Rubbin' my Harry's nose in it like that." She shook her head disgustedly. "Mick Curtis, of all people! That one doesn't know which way is up, Miss Evans!"

Sarah nodded sympathetically. "I'd like to return now to the day of the farmers' shoot, Mr. Settle. Could you tell me what happened, starting from the beginning?"

Settle didn't speak for a few moments, as if he were organizing his thoughts. "It was right foggy that day," he began slowly. "Worst I'd seen it this season. There were fifteen of us, sixteen including Mr. Dinsdale. We managed to get one drive in in t' morning. We broke for lunch around noon and returned to t' shootin' box."

"Who was there at the shooting box, Mr. Settle?" Sarah asked.

"Every one that was on t' moor that mornin'. The missus—" he glanced at his wife "—and Katie Elger were servin' lunch."

"Katie doesn't like shootin'," Mrs. Settle commented.

Sarah nodded. "The results of the postmortem indicate that Mr. Dinsdale had been drinking before his death . . ." She left it open.

Settle scowled. "T' bugger was always drinkin'."

"You shouldn't speak ill of t' dead, Harry!" Mrs. Settle admonished.

Mr. Settle muttered something under his breath.

"Did you see him drinking that day?" Sarah persisted.

"Aye, he had his share of wine at lunch, I reckon."

"What about other times—during the shooting, for instance?"

"I didn't notice, but he usually carried a flask with whisky in it."

"Would you say he was drunk?"

"No more than usual."

"Right, then. What happened after lunch?"

"We went back up on t' East Moor and—"

Sarah looked up from her notebook. "Sorry, East Moor is to the east of Blackamoor Rigg Road, right?"

Settle nodded.

"Please continue."

Settle scratched his head thoughtfully. "T' fog was showin' no sign of lettin' up, so we just stayed in t' butts waitin' for a break. It must of been about a half hour or so when I 'eard two gunshots and then a great bloody kerfuffle comin' from t' far end of t' line of butts. I got down there as fast as I could and found everyone standin' around Mr. Dinsdale." He paused. "It weren't a pleasant sight," he said simply.

"Tell me exactly what you saw, Mr. Settle."

"Mr. Dinsdale lyin' on t' ground, twitchin' summat terrible, 'e was. Katie Elger kneelin' down beside 'im. The rest of t' guns standin' around. Mick Curtis pukin' 'is guts up. And t' bloody adder." His face tightened.

"Had Mr. Dinsdale been unwell any time up to that point?" Sarah asked.

Settle looked at her with an odd expression on his face. "What do you mean, unwell?"

Sarah shrugged easily. "I understand he had asthma; I was just wondering if he'd had an attack that day, that's all."

"Oh, that. He was always huffin' and puffin', but no more than usual, I reckon."

"You're sure?"

"Aye."

She paused briefly to gather her thoughts. "I want to make sure I've got this straight. You said that there were sixteen of you on the shoot, including Mr. Dinsdale. How many butts are there again?"

"Eight on East Moor," Settle answered.

"So there are eight guns in the butts and eight other people driving the grouse?"

Settle nodded. "Except for Mr. Dinsdale. He was always a gun."

"Who determines who's a gun and who's a driver?"

"You mean a beater, lass," Settle corrected.

Sarah grinned. "Right."

"We just divided ourselves up at t' beginnin' of t' day, and those that were beaters in t' mornin' got to shoot in t' afternoon."

Sarah frowned. Something didn't add up. She mused aloud. "If Mr. Dinsdale was always shooting, there would only be seven butts available. Yet you said there were fifteen others including yourself. It seems to me that one person wouldn't get to shoot."

"One of the farmers, Brian Whyte, brought 'is fourteen-year-old boy along. Normally 'e would have had to share a butt with 'is father in t' afternoon, but at t' last minute, one of t' others offered to give up 'is place for t' lad."

This caught Sarah's attention. "Who was that?" she asked.

"A local farmer, name of Frank Elger."

"Mr. Elger would have joined the beaters, then?"

He hesitated for just an instant. "Aye, that's right."

She took a sip of her tea.

"Do have a bit of shortbread, lass," Mrs. Settle urged.

"You won't have to twist my arm, Mrs. Settle," Sarah replied, taking a large piece from the blue willow-patterned plate. She munched away happily for a moment, making appreciative sounds as the buttery shortbread literally melted in her mouth. She tried not to think about her waistline as she helped herself to another piece. She turned to Mr. Settle. "I've been wondering about something. Was it usual for Mr. Dinsdale to participate in the farmers' shoot?"

"It's traditional for t' landlord to 'elp out. Old Mr.

Dinsdale used to beat side-by-side with 'is tenants, but 'e'd never shoot 'imself. 'E felt it was t' farmers' day to 'ave some sport." Mr. Settle screwed up his face in disgust. "Not like 'is bloody son. I think young Mr. Dinsdale came out just to make sure that 'is tenants didn't shoot too many of 'is grouse or drink too much of 'is beer."

"Harry!" Mrs. Settle warned.

"It's t' truth, woman!" Mr. Settle retorted.

In the interests of restoring family harmony, Sarah remarked that the rain seemed to be letting up.

Mr. Settle grunted disinterestedly. Mrs. Settle appeared to be sulking. Her ample bosom rose and fell in time to a clock that was ticking somewhere in the house.

How to broach a prickly subject? Sarah wondered. Once again, she decided it was best to damn the torpedoes. "And you, Mr. Settle," she said, "you say you were no longer working for the estate, yet you participated in the shoot. Why is that?"

He gave her a look that made her feel guilty for asking the question. Before he could speak, Mrs. Settle rose to her husband's defense.

"My Harry's been runnin' t' farmers' shoot for over twenty years, ever since old Mr. Dinsdale took over t' estate. Believe me, Miss Evans, 'e 'ad to swallow 'is pride, but 'e felt it was 'is duty to 'elp out that one last time. It was like 'is retirement due, in a way." She looked at her husband sitting beside her, her eyes moist.

Mr. Settle just stared at his large, callused hands folded on his lap.

Sarah took a deep breath. "How long have you worked as a gamekeeper, Mr. Settle?"

"Goin' on forty years now."

"And how long at Blackamoor?"

"I started 'ere, workin' with my father when Lord Livingston owned the estate."

"You must know these moors like the back of your hand, then."

"Aye, I reckon." A hint of pride in his voice.

"Have you ever heard of anyone being bitten by an adder before?"

"Beasts get bit from time to time, and a walker once on t' West Moor," he said slowly.

"Would you say that Mr. Dinsdale's encounter with the adder was unusual in any way?"

He looked up at her. "Bloody unusual, I'd say."

"Unusual how?" she asked.

He returned to an examination of his hands. "Never 'eard of such a thing," he muttered.

Sarah had concluded by then that she was rapidly approaching the point of diminishing returns and was unlikely to extract any more useful information from the gamekeeper and his wife. She toyed with the idea of bringing up the photograph of the Walkers, but she didn't want the Settles to think she was a snoop. The irony of this concern did not escape her. "I won't take up any more of your time," she said brightly, getting to her feet. "Thank you for the lovely shortbread, Mrs. Settle. I'll never be satisfied with the store-bought variety again."

Mr. and Mrs. Settle stood up in unison and stood together awkwardly.

"Oh, there is just one more thing," Sarah said. "If you

think of anything else, anything at all, you can get in touch with me at the Lion and Hippo."

Mr. and Mrs. Settle glanced at each other, and Sarah could swear that a guilty look passed between them.

CHAPTER 10

"You didn't want them to think you were being nosy. That's bloody rich." Powell chuckled. He sat with Sarah Evans on the outside terrace of the Lion and Hippo, a raised brick patio that adjoined the pub and overlooked the river. The afternoon sun had broken through the clouds and now illuminated the dale with a rich golden light.

She frowned. "You know what I mean. They've been through a lot lately, and it seemed like an invasion of privacy."

"We *are* conducting a police investigation," he pointed out.

She was beginning to get annoyed. "That did occur to me, which is why I decided to broach the subject with Mr. Walker when I got back from the Settles'."

"Brilliant!"

She searched his demeanor for any hint of condescension and, to her relief, could find none. She could forgive many things, but never that. If anything, her companion appeared to be in a slightly manic mood. "As I was saying," she continued patiently, "I had a word with Mr. Walker about the Settles. Mrs. Walker is still suffering from migraine," she added as an aside. "I discovered something rather interesting ... Emma Walker is the Settles' daughter."

Powell sipped his beer with exasperating precision. "I'm not surprised," he said casually. "There's a photograph of the Settles on the desk in the Walkers' office. I noticed it when I first arrived."

Sarah was dumbfounded. "But how could you have known that it was Mr. and Mrs. Settle in the photograph? You've never met them and—" Realization suddenly dawned on her. "How would you like a G-and-T shampoo?"

Powell laughed. "I deserved that. It's a technique I picked up from Merriman: Take credit for everything, and give none to your rivals."

She gave him an odd look. "I wasn't aware that we were rivals."

He met her gaze. "How *would* you characterize our relationship?"

"Er, drinking buddies is closer to the mark, I think."

Powell smiled. "I'd better get us another, then." He got up and walked through the French doors into the pub.

Sarah experienced a whirlwind of conflicting emotions as she looked out over the emerald green fields beyond the river. She could no longer deny that Powell interested her greatly. There was something about him that she found strangely attractive—it was difficult to explain, but he seemed to have a certain intuitive quality that at times was quite disconcerting. She knew, however, that she could never do anything to compromise either herself or her career. She had always been scrupulous in keeping her personal and professional lives separate, and she wasn't about to change now. Neither did she wish to jeopardize her chances of working with him again by complicating their relationship. She chided herself for being so coldly calculating. She knew he was married and her own intuition told her that he was basically a decent bloke, but she would have to be careful not to encourage him. Her reverie was interrupted by Powell returning with the drinks.

"Now, then," he said, "where were we? Ah, yes, you were about to tell me about your conversation with Mr. Walker."

"The whole thing has upset the family terribly, as you can imagine," she began. "Particularly Mrs. Walker. Mr. Walker reckons the stress has brought on her migraine. According to him, the Settles are in a pretty precarious state financially. They've lived in the gamekeeper's cottage all of their married lives—it goes with the job of head keeper, apparently—and they don't have any savings to speak of. Losing their house, their livelihood, has come as quite a blow."

"I take it that Mick Curtis will be moving in as soon as the Settles have vacated the premises?"

Sarah nodded. "There's no love lost between them, I can tell you that. Anyway, they've found a small flat in Scarborough that they can just manage on their pension if they scrimp. The Walkers offered to put them up here or rent a cottage for them in the village, but Mr. and Mrs. Settle wouldn't hear of it. Too proud, apparently."

"A hell of a way to end up," Powell commented. "Anything else?"

She thought for a moment. "There is something . . ." She frowned, as if unsure how to put it into words.

"What is it?" Powell prompted.

She looked at him. "I have a feeling that the Settles are hiding something."

The next morning, Powell drove up to Blackamoor Rigg. He'd given Sarah Evans the task of interviewing the five others who had occupied the butts on East Moor the afternoon of Dinsdale's death. He didn't expect anything new to turn up, but one could never tell, and it would keep his assistant usefully occupied. For his part, he felt as if he needed to tread water on his own for a while, to get his mental bearings.

He pulled off at the car park at the junction of Blackamoor Bank Road with the main road to Eskdale. There was one other car parked there and a man stood on the moor about fifty yards off with a small dog frisking about him. Powell retrieved his trusty Ordnance Survey map from the glove box, unfolded it carefully, and soon located the track leading to the shooting box on East Moor, which took off about a quarter mile down the main road by the looks of it. He decided to walk.

It was a bracing autumn morning and a herd of skittish black-faced sheep were grazing on the grass along the edge of the road. Occasionally a passing car had to toot its horn to hurry a jaywalking beast on its way. He located the track without difficulty and followed it for about a hundred yards up a slight rise and then down into a depression in the moor, in the center of which stood a small stone building with a corrugated metal roof and stovepipe chimney. The door was locked, so he peered through one of the windows into the murky interior. He could see a long wooden table with benches piled on top, a small cooker at one end with shelves and cupboards arranged on either side. He stepped away from the window and walked around the cabin. Approximately twenty-four feet long by sixteen feet wide, rustic but serviceable.

A rough track, consisting of not much more than two muddy ruts, continued past the shooting box in an easterly direction over a slope of burnt heather and disappeared over the skyline. According to the map, the track terminated at the western end of a line of butts that ran on an east-west axis from a point just beyond the shooting box to the crest of the ridge separating Rosedale from Brackendale. Powell reckoned that the westernmost butt must be just out of sight over the rise. The one that was occupied by Harry Settle on the day of the farmers' shoot, he remembered. He decided to retrace Katie Elger's steps as closely as possible when she'd set out in the fog on that fateful afternoon.

He started off on the track and then veered off it to the right, heading southeast as Katie must have done. Eventually he came to a patch of boggy ground. He skirted it and then walked up a gentle slope towards a heather-topped mound silhouetted against the sky. A few seconds later, he could see that the mound was in fact a shooting butt, its low stone walls capped with cut blocks of heather. As he climbed to the crest of the ridge, he was greeted with a most fetching prospect: The green swath of upper Rosedale below him dotted with scattered

red-roofed farms; off to his left the line of grouse butts
with the west side of Brackendale as a backdrop; to
the north and south, as far as the eye could see, an un-
broken expanse of rolling moorland. He could still see
the main road in places, as well as Blackamoor Hall
in the distance.

He consulted his watch. It had taken him a little less
than ten minutes to get to this point after leaving the
shooting box. He recalled that Katie Elger had said that
she'd been wandering about in the fog for about twenty-
five minutes when she heard the gunshots. Given the
poor visibility, she'd no doubt followed a less direct route
than he had, which could explain the time difference.

He walked over to the nearest butt to have a closer
look. Laid out like an H, oriented north and south, so it
could be used to shoot grouse driven from either direction, the drystone walls were about four feet high with
heather growing on top for camouflage. Based on Katie's
account, Powell reckoned that the beaters had been
stationed to the north of the butts on the afternoon in
question. He stepped into the butt.

The ground enclosed by the walls was slightly de-
pressed and covered with short turf. He crouched down
below the heather-topped ramparts then straightened up
and swung an imaginary shotgun in an arc across the sky.
He wondered what it would be like to shoot in the grand
style. He still enjoyed his fishing and the odd bit of rough
shooting, but he had noticed that his appetite for blood
sports had waned in recent years. There had been no
dramatic moment of realization, no ethical or political
transformation, as far as he could tell—there was just
something about the finality of it all that made him in-

creasingly uncomfortable about taking the life of another creature. He was, however, no vegetarian, and had often argued the hypocrisy of the anti–blood sport position— at least as espoused by the majority of its adherents. These were usually the same people who, whilst objecting to the shooting of game for sport, devoured with relish the pallid carcasses of factory chickens bought from their local Sainsburys.

Powell's philosophical musing was suddenly interrupted by the intrusion of a chilling thought. Not that long ago, a human being had lain, alone and helpless where he now stood, suffering an agonizing death. And even more chilling was the possibility that Dinsdale had not been killed by an adder. Powell was becoming convinced that the local police were on to something, but for the wrong reasons. Too many things didn't add up and it was becoming increasingly evident that Dickie Dinsdale had potential enemies. The Settles, the Walkers, the Elgers, for instance—and that was just for starters.

He examined the enclosing stone walls of the butt. The stones fit closely and there didn't appear to be a gap that was more than two inches wide. Hardly big enough for an adder to squeeze through, in his estimation. Nor did there seem to be any place in the wall where a cavity could exist that was large enough for a snake sex orgy (as Sarah had so vividly put it) or even a single individual of the onanistic persuasion. He walked around to the other side of the butt and conducted a similar inspection, with the same result. As he came around to the south side again, he noticed a spent shotgun cartridge on the ground, half concealed in the heather. He picked it up and examined it. An Eley Grand Prix No. 6. He looked around the immediate vicinity and soon found another identical red case. He put them both in his jacket pocket.

Powell set off towards the next butt—the one that had been occupied by Mick Curtis—pacing off the distance. It turned out to be nearly fifty yards away. Far enough that Curtis may well have had difficulty hearing anything of his employer's distress, particularly in light of the fact that Dinsdale was drunk and might not have realized exactly what was happening to him. Powell had a quick look around the butt, which was similar in every respect to the first one, and found nothing of interest. Ahead, the moor began to fall away into Brackendale; he could see the next butt and just the heather top of the one next to that, but the remaining four were hidden from view. When he reached the third butt he looked back; the first two butts were hidden behind a hummock of heather. He continued along the line of butts, making a cursory examination of the next two. From his vantage point, he could see the last four spaced out ahead of him. Up to that point, the distance between the butts had varied from forty to fifty yards.

A movement overhead caught his attention. A hen harrier was circling above him, effortlessly riding the air currents searching for prey. Powell unzipped his jacket and headed for the next butt, keeping an admiring eye on the harrier. If he'd been paying attention to where he was stepping, he might have noticed the wire strung tautly through the heather about six inches off the ground.

As it was, he caught it with the toe of his left boot. A deafening explosion rang in his ears and he experienced an odd sensation of detachment as he went down, everything seeming to happen in slow motion. He found himself lying facedown in the heather with a sharp pain in his right knee. After he realized that he was more or less in one piece, he lay still, his heart pounding wildly, and tried to get his bearings. There wasn't a sound, just the wind rustling in the grass and the acrid smell of cordite. He rolled over with a painful grunt and looked around. No one was in sight. Just his old friend the harrier circling complacently overhead. He looked down at his leg—there was no sign of blood or any obvious damage. Relief suddenly gave way to anger. He swore aloud. He'd probably reinjured his bloody knee—twisted it when he fell. He struggled awkwardly to his feet. The pain wasn't too bad, he decided, so he did an impromptu slow-motion jig to verify his diagnosis. When he was satisfied that his knee was basically sound, he began to look around.

He quickly located the trip wire stretched across the track he'd been following and discovered that it was anchored on the right side, about six feet off the path, by a steel post driven into the ground. He then followed the wire on the other side of the path to a simple device, consisting of a metal tube, pointed skyward, with a shotgun cartridge inserted and a spring-loaded firing mechanism, through which the wire was strung to another steel post.

Wincing slightly, Powell bent down and cocked the firing pin. Then he stood up and tripped the wire with his foot. There was a loud *click* as the spring was released and the striker hit the head of the spent cartridge. "Bloody hell!" he said aloud, feeling slightly foolish. The contraption had obviously been designed to frighten poachers and bring the gamekeeper running. Now that he thought about it, he was rather looking forward to having a word with Mick Curtis.

Limping slightly, he continued down the track, keeping a sharp eye on the ground ahead of him, until he came to the last of the butts. He walked past it another few yards and, as he'd expected, was able to look down on the shooting box. He heard the clashing of gears and the sound of a vehicle coming up the track from the main road. A few seconds later a Land Rover lurched into view.

CHAPTER 11

Powell set off down the track towards the shooting box. The Land Rover had stopped beside it and a man got out. He was carrying a shotgun. Powell waved but the man did not respond. He stared, stone-faced, as Powell approached.

"This is private land," the man said in a belligerent manner, when Powell arrived at the shooting box. "Clear off." Medium build—in his mid-thirties, Powell guessed—with longish blond hair, rugged good looks, and a superior air about him. He was wearing an old waxed jacket and fingerless shooting gloves.

Powell smiled benignly. "Mr. Curtis, I presume? My name's Powell. I believe you spoke to my colleague, Detective-Sergeant Evans."

If Powell had been hoping for a reaction, he was not disappointed. Curtis's demeanor changed instantly.

"I do apologize, Mr. Powell. We've been having problems with poachers lately. I was down the road spreading grit when I heard the warning gun go off and naturally assumed . . ."

"No harm done," Powell said crisply. He declined to point out that he might well have crippled himself as a result of Curtis's booby trap. "But now that you're here," he said, "I would like to have a word, if it's convenient?"

Curtis looked mildly relieved. He broke open his gun and laid it on the seat of the Land Rover. He reached into his right pocket for a set of keys. "Why don't we go inside?" he said.

Powell looked at the gamekeeper across the table. "And you're absolutely certain you didn't hear a sound out of Mr. Dinsdale?"

"Not until I decided to make the rounds. It wasn't until I got to within a few yards of his shooting butt that I heard him sort of groaning, like." Curtis shook his head. "If I'd only checked on him earlier, maybe things would have ended up differently . . ."

"Go on."

Curtis took a deep breath. "I called his name, but he didn't answer. Then I walked around to the back and saw him lying there. It was bloody gruesome, I can tell you. I was about to see if there was anything I could do for him—" he swallowed hard "—when I saw the snake. It was in the corner of the butt near his—near his outstretched hand. I reacted instinctively, I guess, and blew the bloody thing's head off."

"Witnesses heard two shots . . ." Powell observed.

Curtis nodded. "I wanted to make sure."

"At any point did you touch Mr. Dinsdale?"

"No—no, I don't think so. I can't really remember."

"I'm curious, Mr. Curtis. Had you ever seen an adder before?"

"I've seen the odd one sunning itself on the moor."

"Do you remember what happened next?"

Curtis frowned. "It's all a bit of a blur. I remember standing there, just bloody shaking. I have this thing about snakes," he explained. "The next thing I remember is Katie Elger appearing out of nowhere. I was sick after that and don't remember much else. Sorry."

Powell smiled reassuringly. "I understand you got on well with your employer."

"He was a progressive man and he appreciated my ideas. He expressed his confidence in me by appointing me head keeper." It sounded like he was giving an acceptance speech.

"I thought it had something to do with the protest," Powell said.

Curtis stiffened. "Yeah, well, that was just the final straw. Mr. Dinsdale had warned Harry about the protest; he should have been able to head it off."

"Stumpy Macfarlane is a pretty sophisticated operator."

"Whatever. The fact is, old Harry is past it and should have retired years ago," Curtis said coldly.

"You're aware that the local police view Mr. Dinsdale's death as suspicious?"

Curtis nodded soberly.

"Can you think of anyone who might have borne a grudge against him?"

Curtis hesitated. "I suppose it's no secret that Mr. Dinsdale tended to rub some people the wrong way. Like I said, he had a lot of new ideas for Blackamoor and people around here tend to be fairly conservative. But I can't think of anyone who disliked him *that* much."

"What about Harry Settle?"

"Old Harry's basically harmless."

"And Stumpy?"

"I wouldn't put anything past that bastard, but it wouldn't make a lot of sense, would it? His way of getting back at Mr. Dinsdale was to drag his good name through the tabloids."

"Ah, yes, that reminds me. You were there on August twelfth. Perhaps you can tell me exactly what happened between Stumpy and Mr. Dinsdale?"

Curtis folded his arms and stared defiantly at Powell. "I didn't see a bloody thing."

When Powell reached the bottom of Blackamoor Bank he decided on the spur of the moment to follow up on Sarah's visit to the Settles. He crossed the beck and turned into the lane leading to the Settles' cottage. He urged his Triumph along carefully between the ruts and through several mud puddles. As he drew up in front of the cottage yard, a graying, barrel-shaped man, with a black Lab at heel, walked across the yard to meet him.

Powell climbed out of his car and introduced himself. "Mr. Settle, I'm here to ask you a few more questions."

"Oh, aye?" Settle said gruffly. He looked like a man sentenced to be hanged.

A woman's shrill voice called from the door of the cottage. "Who's there, Harry?"

"Never mind, woman!" Settle shouted. Then he stood there, shifting his weight awkwardly from foot to foot. The mud beneath his boots made a queer sucking sound.

Powell smiled. "I see you're raising pheasants, Mr. Settle. Would you mind if I had a look around?"

Settle grunted in a noncommittal manner then turned and trudged across the yard towards the pens in back of the cottage. Powell followed him. By the time they got there, the dog, which had run on ahead, was sniffing eagerly at the enclosing wire mesh of the nearest pen. The milling flock of pheasants, mostly gaudy cocks, clucked and bobbed their heads nervously, ebbing away from the intruders like a green, red, and bronze tide. A few birds flushed wildly and flew with clattering wings to the far end of the pen. There were three pens, the sides and tops enclosed with wire-mesh netting, separated by low privet hedges, each about fifty feet wide and two hundred feet long.

"How many birds do you have here, Mr. Settle?" Powell asked with interest.

"Couple thousand," Settle muttered.

"That seems like quite a few."

"Not like t' old days," the old gamekeeper said grudgingly. "Used to release upwards of fifteen thousand birds on t' estate."

Powell whistled.

"Those were t' grand days," Settle continued, warming to his subject now. "Old Mr. Dinsdale used to bring 'is friends up from Leeds and Sheffield and Newcastle after t' grouse was over. 'E used to like takin' t' high birds, did Mr. Dinsdale."

"I imagine things have changed quite a bit since then," Powell ventured.

"Didn't have electric hens for one thing," Settle said.

"Hatched t' chicks natural like and had less disease because of it." He looked forlornly at the bobbing birds. "Don't know what we'll do with 'em now."

"Did young Mr. Dinsdale like his pheasants high, as well?" Powell asked.

Settle's expression darkened. "That one didn't know if 'e was comin' or goin' 'alf t' time. Ran t' estate into t' bloody ground, 'e did. Just didn't 'ave a 'ead for it. Always cookin' up some 'alf-arsed scheme."

"What kind of schemes, Mr. Settle?"

Settle muttered something unintelligible. Powell gathered from his diatribe that, unlike his former underkeeper, Mick Curtis, the old gamekeeper was not one for the progressive ideas. Time now to change tacks. "I was up on East Moor to have a look at the shooting butts this morning," he began, "and I was wondering about something. Who determines which gun gets which butt?"

"Each butt 'as a number. You draw numbers for t' startin' positions, then t' guns move up two butts for each drive."

"I see. Is that the way it was done for the farmers' shoot?"

"The guns drew for positions in t' mornin', but we only got one drive in. After lunch we switched places. Mr. Dinsdale 'ad already taken 'is place in t' end butt—he allus liked it best—so the rest of us drew for t' other ones."

"Why did he prefer that particular butt?"

Settle screwed up his face and spat. "T' birds like to hug t' drop-off into Rosedale. 'E reckoned 'e got better shootin' in t' end butt."

"Since Mr. Dinsdale was shooting in the afternoon, I

assume he was one of the beaters, along with you and the others, on the morning shoot?"

"'E weren't there in t' mornin'. Turned up at t' shootin' box just afore lunch."

"I see. Mr. Settle, would you be so kind as to write down the names of the beaters in the afternoon?" Powell produced his notebook and pen then, flipping to a back page, handed them to Settle.

The gamekeeper painstakingly wrote down eight names and returned the notebook and pen to Powell.

"Thank you, Mr. Settle. You've been most helpful."

A flicker of relief crossed Settle's face.

"There is one more thing. Sergeant Evans felt that you wanted to tell her something yesterday, but you seemed reluctant for some reason. I think it would be best if you told me now."

Settle stared stolidly at his boots and said nothing.

Powell held his breath. The seconds stretched out like an emotional trip wire. There was a sudden explosion of wings as a pheasant took off, causing Powell to start.

Settle looked up. "Aye," he said slowly, "it's been eatin' away at me, right enough." Then he turned abruptly. "Over here, lad." He led Powell to a small wooden shed with a padlocked door. "It's where I keep t' poisons locked up," he said. "About a week before Mr. Dinsdale's death, someone broke in—prised off t' hasp. I didn't think much of it at t' time. Nowt seemed to be missin'. Reckoned it was just kids."

"What kind of poisons?" Powell asked sharply. Settle's words had surged through him like an electric current.

Settle seemed taken aback by Powell's change of tone. "Pesticides. Chemical for t' sheep dip, weed killer for t' bracken." He scratched his head. "Rat poison. Sprays for t' wife's roses."

"Do you mind if I have a look inside?" Powell asked.

Settle extracted a cluster of keys from his trouser pocket, opened the lock, and removed it from the hasp. Then he swung open the door, stepped into the shed, and switched on the light. Powell followed him. The shed was approximately eight feet by ten feet in size with a dirt floor, windowless, and illuminated by a single naked lightbulb. Bags of fertilizer were stacked in a double row along the left side, the back wall was cluttered with gardening tools, and on a wooden shelf running along the right wall at about shoulder height was a neatly arranged collection of bottles, tins, and cartons. Beneath the shelf on the floor were several larger canisters and a tangle of hoses and spray nozzles.

Powell went over to the shelf and perused the labels. It was enough to make Rachel Carson spin in her grave: Bugs Begone, Kill-O-Weed, Rat-Ex, and numerous others. Nothing like the healthy lifestyle in the unspoiled British countryside. "Are you absolutely certain that nothing was taken, Mr. Settle?"

Settle shrugged. "Not as far as I can tell."

"But you'd have no way of knowing if someone took some pesticide from one of the containers?"

The gamekeeper shook his head.

Powell sighed. "Does anyone else have a key?"

"Just Mick, but like I said, whoever broke in didn't use a key."

Powell removed one of the bottles from the shelf and looked at the label. "What kind of license do you need to use this stuff?"

"Don't need one if you're usin' it on your own or your employer's property."

"Really?" Powell was mildly surprised. He replaced the bottle. "Right. I want to make a list of everything here. Give me a hand, would you?"

They went to work, Settle laboriously reading the label on each container and Powell copying down the product name and list of ingredients.

Twenty minutes later they emerged from the shed. Settle relocked the door then turned to face Powell.

"Why did you decide to tell me about this, Mr. Settle?"

The old gamekeeper set his jaw grimly. "I saw Mr. Dinsdale up on t' East Moor before he died . . ." He paused significantly. "If you're wantin' my opinion, Chief Superintendent, it weren't no snake what was ailin' 'im."

CHAPTER 12

When Powell got back to the Lion and Hippo in the midafternoon, there was no sign of Sarah Evans, so he wandered into the pub for a quick sandwich. He inquired after Mrs. Walker and learned that she was still "under the weather," as Mr. Walker put it. He finished his lunch and went up to his room. He placed a call to London that occupied him for nearly half an hour. Afterward, he lay on his bed and dozed off.

He didn't awake until after six. He showered until he felt half human again and then knocked on Sarah's door, but there was no response. He found her downstairs, chatting with Mr. Walker in the otherwise empty pub.

"We didn't wake you, did we, sir?" she quipped. Then she noticed his slight limp. "What did you do to your leg?"

"It's a long story." Powell grunted as he sat down at the bar beside her. He ordered his usual pint of Tetley's and glanced out the French doors at a bucolic sunlit view. "Order another drink and we'll go outside," he said.

"How was your day?" he asked when they were settled on the terrace.

"Frustrating, if you must know. I managed to track down two of the farmers on our list. I'm still working on the other two. One of them, Brian Whyte, is off at a sheep sale somewhere—should be back tomorrow—and there's no sign of the other one."

Powell tossed her a questioning look. "What do you mean, no sign of him?"

"No one seems to know where he is, not even his wife."

"Which one is it?" he asked, trying to remember the names on the list.

"Bloke named Albert Turner."

"Any indications?"

She shrugged. "I got the impression that he has a drinking problem and may be off on a binge."

Powell took a sip of his beer. "You'd better follow that up. What about the two you did manage to track down?"

"Nothing of interest. They both said they weren't aware of anything amiss until they heard the shots and rushed over to Dinsdale's shooting butt."

"What about the other one—the young lad who took Frank Elger's place?"

"He's the son of the bloke who's at the sheep sale. According to his mum, he's with his dad."

Powell nodded. "I turned up something rather interesting at the Settles' this afternoon," he remarked casually.

This caught her attention. "Really? What were you doing there?" A slight edge had crept into her voice.

He tried to put it as diplomatically as he could. "You

made it pretty clear that you thought the Settles were hiding something. I decided it might be useful to try a different approach. You know, sort of a good cop, bad cop thing," he added.

Her face flushed. "You mean you thought they might spill their guts to someone with more authority, or perhaps someone with a little more experience!"

"It never hurts to try a different tack," Powell said patiently. "As it turns out, you did the groundwork and I simply built on it."

"What did you find out?" she asked grudgingly, curiosity getting the better of her.

"About a week before Dinsdale's death, somebody broke into the shed where Settle keeps the pesticides that are used on the estate. According to Sir Reggie, some of these chemicals are deadly and very difficult to detect."

"Sir Reggie?"

"I called him this afternoon to give him the scoop. I'm trying to convince him to come up. He's mulling it over, but he wants to talk to Dr. Harvey first."

Sarah knew Sir Reginald Quick only by reputation. The Home Office pathologist was widely regarded as an eccentric and formidable genius who did not suffer fools gladly. She had heard through the grapevine that he could make life hell for anyone who had the misfortune to find his or her way into his bad books. And, to his credit, he didn't discriminate in this respect between the brass and the rank and file. She had to admit to herself that she had mixed feelings about the prospect of finally meeting him.

"The situation is basically this," Powell was saying.

"Viewed objectively, the circumstantial evidence suggests that Dinsdale died as a result of being bitten by an adder. This, despite the fact such fatalities are extremely rare and generally only occur if there is an underlying medical condition. We know that Dickie Dinsdale was an asthmatic and suffered from allergies. The bottom line is that the coroner was not convinced either way, which is where we came in." He paused to drain his pint before continuing his analysis. "Don't hesitate to jump in, by the way. Now, the way I see it, the break-in opens up a whole new universe of possibilities. According to Sir Reggie, some of the chemicals in the Settles' storage shed could affect the nervous system in a way that's very similar to snake venom. Interesting, don't you think?"

Sarah looked puzzled. "I'm not sure I follow you. Let's say he *was* poisoned. Isn't it one hell of a coincidence that he got bitten by a snake as well?"

Powell took a drag on his cigarette. "Or supreme bad luck."

"It seems a bit farfetched," she said doubtfully.

Powell looked preoccupied.

"What is it?"

He shook his head irritably. "I don't know. I can't seem to think straight. In any case, we need to consider the possibility. I've been through the list of Dinsdale's personal effects retained by the police as part of the initial investigation. It includes one sterling hip flask. I'll make arrangements with Dr. Harvey to have the contents analyzed straight away. He and Sir Reggie should be able to sort out what to look for. And I'd be interested to know what was on the menu at the shooting box that day."

Sarah nodded. "I'll ask Mrs. Settle."

Powell reached into his shirt pocket and extracted a folded piece of paper. He handed it to her. "I'd like you to check this out."

"What is it?" she asked, unfolding the paper.

"A list of the beaters that were out on the moor that afternoon."

She read the eight names. "It's hardly likely that someone standing in the fog a quarter mile away from Dinsdale's butt would've seen or heard anything," she protested.

He looked at her. "Assuming that's where they all were at the time." He realized that the task he had given her would no doubt be a rote and uninteresting one, but it had to be done. Rank does have its privileges.

Sarah sighed. What a girl had to do to get ahead. "I'll get you another pint," she said.

"Only if you join me."

"I didn't realize that one drank so much in the field."

"Standard procedure, Evans."

She smiled in spite of herself, got up, and went into the pub.

Powell lit a cigarette and smoked thoughtfully.

A few minutes later Sarah rushed back onto the terrace, sans drinks, brandishing a newspaper. Her eyes were wide with excitement. "Look at this!" she said breathlessly. She placed the latest edition of the *Ryedale Times* on the table in front of him. The headline read: NORTH YORK MOORS WATER SCHEME EXPOSED. He quickly skimmed through the story.

The Rydale Times *has learned that prior to his death on September 13, Richard Dinsdale, son of the ailing*

supermarket magnate Ronald Dinsdale, had been in se-
cret negotiations with the Hull Water Corporation in
connection with a proposed scheme to flood the scenic
valley of Brackendale in the North York Moors Na-
tional Park. The allegation was made by Michael Mac-
farlane, the noted environmental activist. Macfarlane,
better known as Stumpy, has conducted numerous
protests around the country, including an attempt to
sabotage a grouse shoot on the Dinsdales' estate in Au-
gust of this year.

According to Mr. Macfarlane, the water project
would involve the construction of a dam on the River
Merlin near the village of Brackendale. The resulting
reservoir would flood the village and the upper portion
of the dale in order to provide drinking water for the
City of Hull. The area in question is part of the Blacka-
moor estate, owned by the Dinsdale family.

A spokesperson for the National Park Authority said
she was unaware of the scheme, whilst Mr. Clive Han-
cock, Senior Engineer for the City of Hull, refused to
either confirm or deny Mr. Macfarlane's allegation.
Mrs. Marjorie Dinsdale, the late Richard Dinsdale's
stepmother, was unavailable for comment at press time.

Another of Dickie's progressive ideas? Powell wondered. He looked up from the newspaper.

"This rather widens the field, doesn't it?" Sarah observed neutrally.

Powell pulled a face. "It never rains but it bloody
pours."

* * *

The next morning, Powell paid a visit to Blackamoor Hall. Once again he was ushered into the study by the skittish Francesca.

Marjorie Dinsdale rose to greet him. "Chief Superintendent, this is an unexpected pleasure," she said, sounding not the least bit pleased.

"I won't beat about the bush, Mrs. Dinsdale. I imagine you've seen yesterday's paper."

She smiled unconvincingly. "Oh, that! That's old news, Chief Superintendent. Just another one of Dickie's brainstorms."

"Would you care to elaborate?"

"Like I told you before, Dickie didn't have a clue about what it takes to run an estate like Blackamoor. Instead of concentrating on doing the basic things properly— modernizing farming methods, improving moorland management, and so on—he was always cooking up some harebrained scheme to make a killing. Dickie was a great one for the quick fix, Chief Superintendent. The Hull water scheme was just the latest in a long line of nonstarters."

Powell was skeptical. "Based on the newspaper article, one gets the impression it had gone beyond being just a twinkle in his eye."

Her face tightened. "He broached the idea with me, and I made it clear to him that I was unalterably opposed to it. He had power of attorney over Ronnie's affairs, so he could basically negotiate with whomever he wished. However, I would never have tolerated such a scheme. There is Ronnie's legacy to consider, not to mention the well-being of the tenants. It's a matter of preserving a way of life, Chief Superintendent. I would have taken Dickie to court to stop him, if it had come to that."

Mrs. Dinsdale had raised an interesting point, which Powell filed away to follow up on later. "I'm wondering what exactly your stepson had in mind, Mrs. Dinsdale. How would putting half the estate under water benefit the family?"

She laughed harshly. "He didn't care about his family. Only his own self-interest." (As she became more agitated, Powell noticed that a definite Cockney flavor had infiltrated her voice.) "He saw the potential for a resort—waterskiing, sailing, fishing, wet bikes roaring about, you get the general idea. He planned to sell the land to the Hull Water Corporation then lease back the rights to develop recreational facilities on the lakeshore. Then he'd turn Blackamoor Hall into a sort of luxury resort hotel. It would have killed poor Ronnie." She looked at Powell impassively. "I wouldn't have allowed that to happen."

"Do you know if anybody else was aware of the scheme?" he asked.

She shrugged. "My daughter, Felicity, knew about it. I have no idea who else Dickie may have told."

Powell formulated his next statement carefully. "I regret to have to tell you that we now believe foul play may have been involved in your stepson's death." He paused to let this sink in, but curiously enough, Mrs. Dinsdale showed no reaction. "I want you to think about this very carefully: Can you think of anyone, anyone at all, who might have benefited from his death?"

"Do you have an hour?" she asked.

"If that's what it takes."

She sighed impatiently. "Let's understand each other, Chief Superintendent. I didn't like Dickie much, and I think the same could be said for ninety percent of the residents of Brackendale. Whether anybody disliked him enough to kill him is a question that you are going to have to answer for yourself."

Powell abruptly got to his feet. "Thank you, Mrs. Dinsdale. You've been most forthright. Don't bother, I'll see myself out."

Forthright or calculating? he wondered as he walked to his car. One thing *was* clear, however: Marjorie Dinsdale was not a woman to trifle with. His train of thought was interrupted by the faint *tok . . . tok . . . tok* of a tennis ball being volleyed. Curiosity got the better of him and he wandered round the side of the house in the direction of the sound.

On a clay court enclosed on two sides by the gritstone facade of the house and an abutting brick wall at the far end, a dark-haired young woman was hitting a tennis ball against the end wall. She was wearing white shorts and sneakers and a skimpy floral top that exposed her midriff. The near end of the court and the side opposite the house were enclosed by a chain-link fence, with a gate in the middle of the long side. Powell walked up to the gate. "Hello there!" he called out.

The woman turned and looked at him. She did not seem particularly surprised at having her practice interrupted. She walked languidly over to where he was standing on the other side of the gate. "Hi, I'm Felicity," she said brightly, tossing her long hair behind her. "And I already know who you are. I was wondering when you'd look me up."

Felicity Jamieson was a stunning young woman, whose sporting attire left little to the imagination, but, to his credit, Powell did his best to keep his mind on task. His attention, however, was drawn inexorably to her pierced navel with its silver stud and, despite his best intentions, he couldn't help wondering how far her penchant for body piercing extended. "Er, may I have a word?" he asked.

She smiled. "I'd love to." She unlatched the gate and swung it open. There was a wooden bench set along the inside of the fence. She sat down and invited Powell to do the same. She crossed her long legs and waited, gazing at him with cool blue eyes.

"You sounded as if you were expecting me, Ms. Dinsdale."

"I'll never forgive you if you don't call me Felicity," she said.

Powell smiled. "All right, Felicity. But you haven't answered my question."

"I figured you'd want to talk to me about my dear departed stepbrother."

Touching. "Why don't you tell me all about him, then?"

"Wouldn't you rather winkle it out of me, Chief Superintendent?" she asked archly.

Powell was mildly perplexed by the young woman— leaning as he did towards the Darwinian side of the nature-nurture argument—since Felicity seemed so unlike her mother, as different as Dickie and his father were from all accounts. A diversionary tactic appeared to be in order. "Tell me something, Felicity. How does a

London girl like you come to be living in the North York Moors?"

She shook her head wonderingly. "I ask myself that question every day," she said. "Mummy used to work as a legal secretary for Ronnie's solicitor in London. Bloke named Newbury. Ronnie came in one day and one thing led to another, you might say. The next thing I knew, I found myself in this drafty old pile in the middle of nowhere. I was sixteen at the time—if I'd known better, I wouldn't have come."

"There are worse things than living in the country," Powell observed dryly.

"Yeah, well, the club scene sort of sucks," she replied, without a hint of sarcasm.

"Why do you stay then?"

She appeared to ponder this for a moment. "You can get used to anything, I suppose. And there's less competition for blokes."

"I understand that Dickie had plans to liven the place up."

"Oh, the resort thing. Dickie always had big plans. I never paid much attention to him." She was beginning to look bored.

"Do you know if anyone outside the family knew about his latest project?"

She shrugged lightly. "I dunno."

"Did you tell anyone?"

"I can't remember." She idly twisted a strand of hair round and round her finger.

Powell sighed inwardly. "Is there anything else you'd care to tell me, Felicity?"

She looked at him with those expressionless blue eyes. "I want you to know that Dickie was a frigging pervert," she said in a voice oddly devoid of emotion. "He used to have it off, spying on me having sex with my boyfriends."

CHAPTER 13

Robert Walker was just opening up the pub when Powell arrived back at the inn. He inquired after Sarah and learned that she had gone up to Dale End Farm. Walker seemed uncharacteristically subdued.

"Tell me, Mr. Walker, what do think of this water scheme I read about in the paper yesterday?"

"First I'd heard of it," he said quickly. "But I wouldn't have put it past him. Flood the whole bloody dale and screw the tenants, that was his style."

"Do you think they'll still go ahead with it?" Powell asked, testing the figurative waters.

"You tell me. Mrs. Dinsdale seems like a decent sort, but I imagine there's quite a bit of money involved . . ."

Powell looked puzzled. "I must admit to being a bit surprised that word of the scheme didn't leak out before this."

Walker blinked slowly. "Yeah, well, I expect these sorts of things are kept pretty hush-hush."

Powell wasn't convinced that Walker was being entirely forthright. "Mr. Walker, what exactly would happen to the estate's tenants—the farmers, people in the village like yourself—if the land were to be sold?"

Walker shrugged. "There would have to be some compensation, of course, but, for most of us, it wouldn't be nearly enough to pick up and start all over again."

"If word of Dinsdale's negotiations with the water company *had* leaked out, how do you suppose people in Brackendale would have reacted?"

"I can only speak for myself, Chief Superintendent."

"Yes?"

Walker's expression was emotionless. "I would have done everything I could to stop him."

Powell decided to drive up to Dale End Farm to see if he could intercept Sarah. They had much to talk about before he could finalize his plans for an excursion to York the next day. He climbed into his TR4 and turned the ignition switch. Nothing happened save an ominous and all-too-familiar *click*. He held his breath and tried it again with the same result. Cursing creatively, he put the car in gear, got out and rocked it backward and forward. He climbed back in and turned the switch. *Click*. Before he could feel too sorry for himself, he recalled the assertion of an American friend that the reason Brits drink warm beer is because the inner workings of their refrigerators are manufactured by the same firm that makes electrical parts for their cars.

The man at the garage nodded sagely. "Aye, sounds like t' starter, all right. T' worm gear's probably jammed on t' flywheel. Any road, tomorrow's Sunday, so I won't be able to get t' parts until Monday."

Powell sighed. It was just what he needed. "Fine. Here's the keys. Do you need a hand pushing it over here?"

The mechanic grinned toothlessly. "It's all part of t' service, sir."

As Powell walked back to the Lion and Hippo, he wondered how much this latest chapter in the long, sorry tale of his obsession with impractical and unreliable cars was going to set him back. At the very least, he would have to alter his travel plans. When he got back to the inn, Sarah's black Vauxhall was back in the car park.

"That is a shame," Sarah said when she heard about Powell's car. "And British racing green is such a lovely color," she added innocently.

Powell scowled. "I'll need a lift to the train station in Malton, first thing in the morning." He explained about his planned visit to York. "In the meantime, I've got some phone calls to make. What's on your agenda this afternoon?"

She smiled ruefully. "I'm still going through my to-do list. "

"I'm afraid I've come up with a few more things to add to it." He smiled. "We'll have a strategy session this evening, after we've both done a proper day's work."

Powell went up to his room, rang up Detective-Sergeant Black, and issued a series of instructions relating to Ronnie Dinsdale's London solicitor. He then managed to track down Sir Reggie in his garden in Hampstead.

"Do you realize it's a bloody weekend, Powell?" Sir Reggie thundered.

Powell could imagine Sir Reggie hurling his mobile phone into the compost heap if he wasn't handled carefully. "I do apologize, Reggie." (The senior Home Office pathologist refused to be addressed by his title, at least by those he got on with—unlike Merriman, who reveled in his own like a dog rolling in a rotting carcass.) "I just thought I'd touch base to see if you'd given any further thought to my invitation," Powell said casually. "I'm traveling down to York tomorrow—I could pick you up at the station. You could catch an afternoon train, if it's convenient."

An ominous silence on the other end of the line, followed by snatches of muffled conversation then a raised feminine voice. A few moments later Sir Reggie was speaking in the manner of a conspiratorial whisper. "As a matter of fact, I *had* decided to lend a hand. I wasn't going to leave until Monday morning, but my wife has planned some infernal dinner party tomorrow evening that I'd just as soon avoid. I've told her that an emergency has arisen in connection with the case, requiring me to change my plans and leave a day early, so mum's the word, eh, Powell? I'll be on the three o'clock train." He rang off.

Powell smiled. A personality strong enough to intimidate Sir Reggie didn't bear thinking about. Feeling at loose ends—and a trifle guilty for leaving Sarah to toil alone in the fields—he decided to spend the rest of the afternoon making inquiries around the village.

* * *

That evening, the pub was as busy as Powell had seen it. A number of couples were seated on the terrace, so Powell and Sarah Evans secluded themselves in the snug, where they might have a measure of privacy.

Sarah was warming to her subject. "According to Katie Elger, most of the time there was some dispute going on between Dinsdale and his tenants. If he wasn't accusing someone of poaching or stealing, he was raising the rents or just generally making life difficult. Katie thinks he was trying to force the farmers off their land so he could redevelop the estate for commercial purposes. The Hull Water Corporation scheme seems to bear her theory out."

"It's certainly consistent with what we've been hearing over and over again, which always makes me suspicious. What did her father have to say about all of this?"

"Not much."

"Did you ask him about the afternoon of the farmers' shoot? Why he changed places with that farmer's son?"

She nodded. "It was the lad's first time, apparently. Mr. Elger was just being kind, I think."

Powell grunted neutrally. "Did he mention seeing or hearing anything unusual?"

"From what I've been able to gather so far, the beaters remained in position on the moor during the critical period. The idea was that as soon as the fog lifted they'd be able to start the drive quickly. They would have been thirty or forty yards apart, out of sight of each other, and at least a quarter mile in front of the butts. Mr. Elger says he heard the two shots and wondered about it at the time but didn't do anything. He said that he heard some of the other beaters talking back and forth about it."

"Do you know if he talked to any of the other beaters?"

"He says they met briefly as a group when Mick Curtis dropped them off at the starting point after lunch and again afterward when Harry Settle showed up to tell them what had happened to Dinsdale. So far, I've managed to track down three of the other beaters and they all tell basically the same story."

"So it's possible that any one of them could have been just about anywhere at the critical time?"

Sarah frowned. "I suppose."

Powell emptied his pint. "Any news of our missing farmer?"

She shook her head. "I've asked around; apparently it's not the first time he's gone off on a bender for a few days."

Powell grunted. "My round, I think." He returned in a few moments with another pint and a glass of white wine. "You know what puzzles me about this business, Sarah?"

"What's that?"

"That someone didn't do for old Dickie a long time ago. The only person I've met so far who's had a good word to say about him is Mick Curtis, and that's only because Curtis was rewarded by Dinsdale at Harry Settle's expense. Not only was Dinsdale a mean-spirited, incompetent Peeping Tom, it now comes to light that he was making plans to destroy half of Brackendale and a traditional way of life, for his own profit."

"Charming character," Sarah remarked.

"Furthermore, a storeroom containing a plethora of toxic pesticides is broken into a week before Dinsdale dies of suspicious symptoms that resemble poisoning. Up on the moor in the fog where no one knows where the hell anyone else is. It's just too bloody perfect."

Sarah frowned. "If it hadn't been for the adder, I'd be inclined to agree with you."

He looked at her. *"Latet anguis in herba,"* he said.

"I beg your pardon?"

"Virgil. Beware the snake in the grass."

Sarah raised a suspicious eyebrow. "This isn't the first time you've spoken to me in a dead language. I'm beginning to wonder about you."

"A vestige of the education I spent so much of my life acquiring in order to prepare myself for a life as a copper."

She laughed then took a sip of her wine. "What's next?"

"I've asked Bill Black to look up Ronnie Dinsdale's solicitor in London. Felicity let his name slip. Evidently, Mrs. Dinsdale used to be his secretary. I'm interested in the content of old Dinsdale's will. For instance, who inherits the estate now that his son is dead? His lawyer doesn't have to tell us anything, of course, but I'm hoping he'll be cooperative. Secondly, I've got great hopes for Sir Reggie. If we can just nail down whether Dinsdale was poisoned . . ."

"And for me?"

"Carry on with your list of witnesses. And you can add one more name to it: Francesca, the dark-eyed servant at Blackamoor Hall. She's constantly skulking around in the background looking guilty about something. Find out if she knows anything. And, oh yes, I'd like you to make some inquires about Felicity Jamieson. I get the impression that she, er, rather likes to put it about a bit."

Sarah shook her head in disbelief. "Why is a woman who likes the company of men always characterized as some sort of tart? If it's a man playing the field, he's just being a lad, isn't he? Nudge, nudge, wink, wink."

"Ouch! I simply wish to explore the possibility that one of her boyfriends may have objected to her step-brother's penchant for watching, that's all."

Sarah blushed. "Sorry, I should have thought of that."

Powell laughed. "Chalk it up to experience." He got up and picked up their glasses.

She looked doubtful. "What time did you say you wanted to leave tomorrow?"

"It's Saturday night!" Powell protested. "Just one more for the road?"

She smiled at him. "All right."

Sitting in this fine public house with a highly agreeable companion, and viewing the world through an imperfect filter of best Yorkshire bitter, it was easy enough to forget that his wife was planning to abandon him for a year, not to mention the fact that the person he despised most in the entire Metropolitan Police Service was poised to take over the top job. Why shouldn't he let his hair down once in a while? He watched Sarah sipping her wine and wondered what she was thinking. "Penny for your thoughts," he said, as precisely as he could manage it.

"I was just wondering if you had any words of wisdom for someone like me who's just starting out."

He wagged his finger reprovingly. "Shop talk."

She smiled ruefully. "Guilty as charged."

"Words of wisdom? Let me see . . ." He thought about it for a moment. "The world," he said presently, "is an unbearably sad place for a policeperson."

She eyed him warily, not knowing whether he was serious. "A policeperson?"

He stared into his glass. "I started writing a novel, you know. I met a writer recently who inspired me to try my hand at it." He looked up at her. "I suppose I felt the need to do something creative, to leave something behind a little more enduring than a legacy of departmental memoranda detailing the pros and cons of the latest reorganization proposal or something equally inane."

"I think I get the idea," she said wryly.

"Anyway," he continued, "I started writing this novel. After I'd roughed out the first few chapters, I made the mistake of letting someone whose opinion I value have a look at it. You know what she said?"

"What?"

"She said it read like it was written by someone who'd learned their English from P. G. Wodehouse." He screwed up his face. "The thing is, I didn't know whether to take it as a criticism or a compliment."

Sarah burst out laughing. "What's it about, this book of yours?"

Powell sighed. "Water under the bridge."

"Come on," she teased, "you can tell me."

"That's what it's about. How you can't turn back the clock. How our individual lives are simply a microcosm of the larger expanding universe."

She shook her head in amazement. "What made you decide to become a cop, anyway?"

"That," Powell said, "is a long story, which I won't bore you with. Let's just say that a degree in classics, followed by a brief and unpleasant taste of army life, didn't equip me for much else."

"You'd have made a good teacher."

"Do you really think so?"

She brushed a strand of hair from her forehead. "I've learned a lot during the short time we've worked together."

He searched her eyes for meaning. "That's because you're an exceptional student," he said.

She cleared her throat. "Yes, well, I think it's important in any professional relationship for both parties to hold up their end. Don't you agree, sir?" She felt like a festering idiot.

Powell finished his beer. "I couldn't have put it better myself, Sergeant." He consulted his watch. "I'm afraid it's getting past my bedtime."

Back in his room, Powell thought about calling Marion but decided it wouldn't be prudent under the circumstances. Later, in bed, he lay thinking about Sarah Evans. Eventually he turned over, disgusted with himself. Christ, he thought, I'm a pathetic, self-centered bastard. Whatever her reasons, whether knowingly or not, he realized that Detective-Sergeant Sarah Evans had done him a good turn that night.

CHAPTER 14

Sarah Evans dropped Powell at the rail station in Malton just before nine-thirty. They hadn't spoken much during the drive from Brackendale, each absorbed in their own thoughts. As they crossed over the River Derwent, Powell was seized with a sense of foreboding that he was at a loss to explain. The feeling remained with him during the short journey to York, and when his train pulled into the station, he decided to walk to Heslington, a distance of about two miles. He had a good hour until his appointment near the university and his head badly needed clearing.

The University of York, founded in 1963 on an estate at Heslington, consisted of a collection of unremarkable concrete blocks—housing colleges and lecture halls, a central hall, and a library—scattered over a wide area around a man-made lake. Powell's destination was Gwyneth House, a student residence on Thief's Lane adjacent to the campus. He located the redbrick building without too much difficulty, scanned the directory beside the door, and pushed one of the buttons.

The intercom crackled. "Who is it?"

"Mr. Macfarlane? It's Chief Superintendent Powell."

The lock buzzed and clicked open. Powell climbed the stairs to the second floor and knocked on the door of Number 23. "Come," a voice called out.

Powell opened the door and entered the room. A slight young man with short, ochre-colored hair was sitting at a computer desk typing on the keyboard. He looked around. "Have a seat," he said. "I'm almost done."

Working on your latest tract? Powell wondered. He sat down on one of three wooden chairs arranged in the center of the room around a small oval table cluttered with papers, a calendar of graduate courses, a textbook titled *Statistical Concepts in Animal Ecology*, a half-full teacup, and a piece of dry toast. He took in his surroundings. Typical student digs: along one wall a single bed and washstand; along the other, the desk and a makeshift bookshelf-cum-stereo-stand, consisting of planks supported by concrete building blocks. Opposite the door, a west-facing window provided a distant view of the ever-present Minster. The walls were decorated with posters as well as a number of framed photographs, some of them signed, showing a more familiar Stumpy, with beard and long hair, along with various other people, several of whom looked vaguely familiar. One of them in particular caught Powell's eye—a smiling older woman standing with her arm around Stumpy. He squinted, trying to make out the woman's face. Bloody hell, he realized, it's Bridget Bardot!

Powell's inventory was interrupted a moment later

when Stumpy got up from his desk, walked over to the table, and sat down opposite him. "You mentioned on the phone that you wanted to talk to me about Dickie Dinsdale," he said breezily. "Do I need to call my lawyer?"

"I don't think that will be necessary, do you?"

"That depends on why you're here, doesn't it?"

Powell flipped open the textbook. "What are you studying, Stumpy? Anarchy 101?"

Stumpy shook his head, as if in amazement. "You're all the bloody same, aren't you? As matter of fact, I'm doing a masters degree in biology. Not that it's any of your business."

"I'll come right to the point; I want to know what happened between you and Dinsdale at Blackamoor on August twelfth."

"Why should I tell you anything?"

"Because," Powell said, "I think Dinsdale was murdered. And I think you can assist us in our inquiries."

Stumpy sneered. "I'm not interested in helping the police. You've never done a frigging thing for me."

"I think his death had something to do with the Hull Water Corporation's scheme to flood Brackendale," Powell persisted. "With Dinsdale out of the way, the project isn't likely to go ahead." He looked blandly at Stumpy. "A victory for the environment, you might say."

Stumpy flushed. "What are you insinuating?"

Powell shrugged. "You tell me."

Having temporarily regained his composure, Stumpy leaned back in his chair. "You know I don't have to tell you anything, but you're so far off the mark, I'm finding it difficult to resist the temptation to set you straight."

"I'm a big boy," Powell said equably. "I can take it."

Stumpy eyed him shrewdly. "Am I a suspect?"

"I've no reason to suspect you of anything at this point," Powell answered truthfully. "If I change my mind, I'll caution you as required by law."

Stumpy laughed bitterly. "The law's an ass. I get the shit kicked out of me for staging a peaceful protest on Dinsdale's grouse moor and *I'm* the one who gets charged."

"It didn't turn out very well for Dickie either."

"Very clever, Chief Superintendent, but you needn't patronize me. I said I'd tell you about it."

"Why don't you start from the beginning, then?"

"A few months ago," Stumpy began, "I got wind of a proposal to dam the River Merlin in upper Brackendale to create a water supply reservoir for the City of Hull. I learned that the Hull Water Corporation had approached Dinsdale to see if he'd be willing to sell them the land they needed for the project. I was appalled, of course." He was becoming increasingly animated. "A private bloody company proposing to destroy one of the few unspoiled areas left in the country for profit. In a frigging national park, for Christ's sake." He glared at Powell. "You know what gets me about the neo-Thatcherite apologists for privatization that continue to run this country—and this latest lot are no better than the others—is their complete and utter moral bankruptcy. The triumph of blinkered ideology over responsibility to the people. They've basically sold the family silver at boot-sale prices, and despite the tedious rhetoric about lean and mean government and the so-called

British entrepreneurial renaissance, the frigging trains don't even run on time anymore. If that's democracy, I'll take anarchy," he concluded pointedly.

Powell was not unsympathetic to Stumpy's position, but that was neither here nor there. "You mentioned that the Hull Water Corporation had approached Dinsdale . . ." Powell prompted.

"Yeah, at that point I had no idea what his position was, so I—"

"How did you find out about this in the first place?" Powell interrupted.

Stumpy regarded Powell warily. "It's not relevant."

"I'll be the judge of that."

Stumpy seemed about to protest but evidently thought better of it. He shrugged. "I heard about it from an old girlfriend of mine, Chloe Aldershot. Her father, Lord Aldershot, is on the board of directors of the Hull Water Corporation. She got wind of it somehow."

Was Stumpy's apparent reluctance to involve Chloe due to a sense of chivalry or something else? This was the same girlfriend, Powell remembered, who had provided Stumpy with an alibi for the day of the farmers' shoot. He wondered what Lord Aldershot thought about his daughter fraternizing with the likes of Stumpy.

"As I was saying," Stumpy continued, "I initially got in touch with Dinsdale to feel him out. He was right pissed off when he realized who I was. It was obvious that he was promoting the scheme and hoped to make a tidy profit in the bargain. I tried to reason with him, pointing out that there was no way the public would tolerate the desecration of the North York Moors. He told me in no uncertain terms to mind my own business." He smiled humorlessly. "The little bastard didn't know who he was dealing with. Before he hung up on me, I basically told him that I was going to stop him, one way or the other."

"When did this conversation take place?"

"Late June, early July."

"I'm a bit puzzled. Why didn't you go public at that time?"

"He would have denied the whole thing, as would the Hull Water Corporation. Then when the deal was signed, it would have been too late to do anything about it. I figured that the best approach would be to take some kind of direct action that would dissuade Dinsdale from proceeding with his plans. That's where the idea of a protest on his grouse moor came from."

"A shot across his bow, so to speak," Powell commented.

"Exactly. A taste of things to come if he didn't forget about the water scheme."

"I understand that you even warned him of your intentions."

Stumpy laughed. "That was a great touch, don't you think? Look, I'm no bloody amateur—I'd planned the thing down to the last detail and I knew there was nothing he could do to stop me. Tipping him off in advance simply made the impact that much greater."

"But you must have known you'd get arrested."

Stumpy looked slightly disappointed in Powell. "All the more publicity to set the stage for the next phase if Dinsdale didn't back down."

Powell had to hand it to him—old Stumpy didn't miss a trick. "Getting back to the August twelfth protest, I am interested in hearing how you pulled it off."

Stumpy smiled, clearly enjoying himself now. "I don't

think I'd be giving away any trade secrets if I told you. It was a piece of cake, really. Dinsdale probably expected us to come marching over the horizon, but I had other ideas. There were six of us altogether, and the problem was how to conceal ourselves in the thick of things until just the right moment. I hit upon the idea of digging into the moor—in foxholes, like. We started a week before the shoot, working at night and carrying the spoil away. During the day, we left our work covered up with plywood sheets camouflaged with blocks of cut heather. I don't mind saying that it worked brilliantly."

Powell had to admit that it had been an audacious plan, but hadn't Stumpy cut his teeth as an activist in the environmental movement by living in tunnels dug in the path of various road improvement projects around the country? "I understand that the local police showed up in due course to take matters in hand," he said.

Stumpy's expression darkened. "Yeah, well, we know whose side *they* were on, don't we?"

"You *were* breaking the law," Powell pointed out.

"I told you before what I think of the frigging law."

Powell ignored this. "Why don't you tell me exactly what happened?"

"They rounded up my crew and left me behind with Dinsdale and the local inspector—Braughton, his name is. When there were no witnesses, Dinsdale knocked me down." He glared at Powell. "Braughton just stood there." He paused. "Then Dinsdale pointed his shotgun at me and fired."

"He must have been a terrible shot," Powell remarked sardonically.

"Very frigging funny." Stumpy was indignant now.

"How was I to know that it wasn't loaded? Psychological abuse, I call it."

"You and your associates were charged with criminal trespass, and you subsequently brought charges against both Dinsdale and the North Yorkshire police related to these alleged abuses."

"Yeah, that's right."

Time to take the upper hand, Powell decided. "You described the August twelfth protest as setting the stage for the next phase of your campaign against Dinsdale. What did you have in mind?"

"I already told you."

"Tell me again."

Stumpy sighed irritably. "If he didn't change his mind, I'd turn up the pressure and go public when the time was right."

"He didn't change his mind though, did he, Stumpy?"

"Like I said, I had a contingency plan."

"Did your plan include killing him?"

Stumpy leapt to his feet. "What a load of arse!" he shouted. "I'm calling my frigging lawyer!"

Powell stood up and faced him, a bland expression on his face. "That is your right, of course," he said. "For the time being, I don't have any further questions, but I may need to talk to you again."

There was a telephone in the entrance hall of the student residence. Powell placed a call to Chloe Aldershot, Stumpy's girlfriend—or was she an ex-girlfriend?—but there was no answer. He rang for a taxi.

After arriving back in the city center, he soon located a large, attractive pub opposite the city wall. He ordered a pint of Theakston's Old Peculiar and a ploughman's to see him through. Sitting at a table near the window, he reflected on his interview with Stumpy. The environmental activist came across as a highly motivated young man who was fanatically dedicated to his cause. His track record in blocking environmentally questionable developments through direct action was impressive. The question was, how far was he willing to go?

While Powell could never countenance breaking the law, he saw a place for dissidents like Stumpy, if only to keep the Merrimans of the world honest, or at least on their toes. As a policeman, he had subjected himself to considerable soul-searching on the question of civil disobedience. If the cause was sufficiently just or noble, one should theoretically be able to act ethically by flouting the law, if that is what was required to redress the perceived wrong. The problem is, there are as many points of view on any given issue as there are people, and nowadays it seems that just about everyone feels aggrieved by someone or something. The chaos that would ensue if every person who felt hard done by took the law into their own hands didn't bear thinking about. There were times, however, when Powell wondered if his desire for stability and order was largely a reaction to the turmoil in his own life.

He stared into his glass, searching the dark bitter for inspiration. His mental meanderings had not entirely diverted his attention from the fact that something about Stumpy Macfarlane was bothering him. He frowned. It was as if the thought were being sucked under the surface of his consciousness by the whirlpool of impressions swirling around in his head. It had something to do with Chloe Aldershot, he was certain of that. He glanced out the window. A van was pulling into the car park. Suddenly, it struck him.

CHAPTER 15

That night in the transport cafe just outside of York on his way to Brackendale, there had been a young couple sitting in the booth next to him. Powell hadn't recognized the man at the time—the closely cropped orange hair was so unlike his trademark beard and dreadlocks—but it was Stumpy, all right. And he was prepared to bet his pension that the woman with him had been Chloe Aldershot. He remembered that neither of them had looked very happy at the time, and he couldn't help wondering why. He drained the last of his pint. Perhaps Ms. Aldershot would be able to enlighten him on that score.

Outside the pub, he tried her number again, but there was still no answer. He checked the time—he had a few hours to kill before it was time to meet Sir Reggie's train. He drew a deep breath. The city seemed to sparkle in the afternoon sun. A stroll along the ancient city wall and then a shufty round the Minster seemed like just the ticket. As he crossed the street, he wondered idly how Sarah Evans was getting on with her list.

The three o'clock train from King's Cross pulled into York at two past five. Powell need not have been concerned about locating his colleague in the throng of travelers returning home from London. When Powell arrived to collect him, the large untidy pathologist was standing in the middle of the platform like an immovable boulder, around which the stream of passengers eddied and flowed. Sir Reggie spotted him and bulldozed his way over.

"Hello, Reggie."

Sir Reggie almost looked glad to see him. "Powell, you have no idea what a close scrape it was."

"I beg your pardon?"

"My wife's a member of the Hampstead Amateur Players," he explained ruefully. "She's laid on a buffet dinner for the lot of them at our place tonight, to be followed by a dress rehearsal of their latest production—" his large red face grew a shade paler "—*The Sound of* bloody *Music*, if you can believe it!"

Powell did his best to imagine a cast of matronly ladies and well-padded gentlemen as the von Trapp children.

"And that's not the worst of it," Sir Reggie continued in a flat voice. He paused dramatically. "My wife is playing the role of Maria. For the past few weeks the house has been alive with the sound of screeching. I hardly get a moment's peace."

Powell bit his tongue. "Er, I see."

"That's neither here nor there now," the pathologist

said gruffly. "But I'm so bloody grateful, I'm going to treat you to one of your damn curries tonight." He fixed Powell with a penetrating glare. "I hope you realize what a sacrifice I'm making—tomorrow I'll be dragging myself all galley-arsed over the moors. Now let's go somewhere where we can chew the fat."

"An intriguing possibility," Sir Reggie admitted, using the back of his hand to wipe a trickle of red wine from his chin. "The thing is, one wouldn't necessarily be looking for signs of homicidal poisoning in a case like this. After all, the chap *was* bitten by a venomous snake, that much is clear. Harvey's a good man. If I'd been doing the post-mortem myself, I'd not likely have gone much further than he did. It is true, however, that an adder bite is not a very likely candidate for the cause of death, even considering that your chap was prone to allergies. Hand over those crisps, would you?"

Powell complied. "I keep wondering if the snake is some sort of red herring," he muttered.

Sir Reggie crunched away noisily. "I'll ignore your mixing metaphors for the moment. But you're not seriously suggesting that someone poisoned Dinsdale, then rounded up an adder and ordered it to bite him?"

Powell shook his head in exasperation. "I don't know whether I'm coming or going on this case. I just know that something is not bloody right."

"In any case," Sir Reggie said, "on your list we've got everything from a rodenticide containing sodium cyanide to insecticides that act by poisoning the nervous system. I've had a chat with Harvey about the case and he's having a comprehensive GC-MS screening, as well as some additional analysis, done on the contents of the victim's flask and on the blood, urine, and liver samples retained at postmortem. We should have the results in a couple days. If there's anything there, we'll find it." He tilted his wineglass significantly.

"I'll get you another." Powell went up to the bar and soon returned with a glass of wine and a pint.

The pathologist sniffed loudly at the glass. "Passable plonk," he pronounced. "Now then, where was I? Oh, yes—the problem, as I see it, is timing. As far as we know, the victim was in good form at lunchtime?"

Powell nodded.

"Most insecticides—the organophosphates, for instance—would take several hours to act. Let's say, for the sake of argument, that Dinsdale was given something at lunch. After that he is ensconced in his shooting butt, and some thirty minutes later he's discovered by his gamekeeper in a coma. Is that the sequence of events?"

"As far as we know."

"Right. An hour for lunch, perhaps a little longer. Let's say an hour on the moor—half an hour to get settled, then half an hour alone. So we need something that would act within a couple of hours and—"

"Why couldn't a poison have been administered hours or even days earlier?"

Sir Reggie cocked a skeptical eyebrow. "That's possible, of course. But it would be damn tricky to time the thing so that the victim would be stricken when he was alone in the shooting butt, assuming that was the idea."

"That's been bothering me, as well," Powell said. "If

it hadn't been for the fog, Dinsdale might have been discovered earlier and perhaps saved. How could the murderer—if that's what we're dealing with—have predicted the weather?" he asked rhetorically.

"Then there's the matter of taste and odor," Sir Reggie added. "It would be difficult to disguise the presence of most insecticides in a flask of whisky."

"Hmm. Is there anything else that fits the bill, then?"

"Cyanide is a possibility, I suppose. It acts by paralyzing the vital functions. Death from prussic acid can occur in a matter of seconds. Cyanide salts—like the sodium cyanide we're dealing with here—take longer to act, relying on the gastric juices in the stomach to break them down and release hydrocyanic acid."

"I should have thought you could detect cyanide poisoning at postmortem."

"Not necessarily. The pathologist had no reason to suspect it in this case. There was, after all, a smoking gun—or at least a hissing snake. Ha ha!"

Powell flashed the obligatory smile.

"There are, in actual fact, few visible signs of cyanide poisoning," Sir Reggie continued, "although the skin may show an irregular cherry red discoloration similar to the effect of carbon monoxide poisoning. But you also see the same thing on bodies that have been exposed to cold temperatures. From lying about on a grouse moor, for instance."

Powell was not satisfied. "But what about the characteristic smell of bitter almonds?"

"The odor you are referring to *may* be detected at the mouth or in the chest and abdominal cavities. However, it's estimated that at least twenty percent of the population are unable to register the smell." Sir Reggie absently ran his hand through his mop of white hair as if to straighten it, but to no effect.

Powell wondered if Sir Reggie was to some extent covering for Dr. Harvey. "It would seem from what you're saying that cyanide is the most likely candidate, then."

The pathologist smiled ghoulishly. "There is one other rather intriguing possibility: fluoroacetamide. It's another rodenticide. It hasn't been approved for use in the UK for a number of years now, but it's not that surprising to find some of it still lying around. Fluorobane, the formulation on your list, is a granular bait, three percent active ingredient in a cereal base. A little water is added to make a delectable slurry, something like porridge."

"Difficult to mask in a flask of whisky," Powell commented.

Sir Reggie grunted. "A bit lumpy, I should imagine. But the thing is, fluoroacetamide is extremely toxic and damned difficult to detect. The symptoms, which start after thirty minutes or so, are fairly nonspecific: vomiting, convulsions, and, eventually, cardiorespiratory failure. And the acute lethal dose is so small—a few hundred milligrams, perhaps—that one would be hard-pressed to detect its presence in the tissues. An ideal poison in every respect," he concluded.

Powell frowned, recalling his conversation with Harry Settle. "According to the gamekeeper, you don't even need a license or permit to use these things."

Sir Reggie shook his head. "That's not strictly true. Before nineteen-eighty-six, pesticides were approved in this country under various voluntary schemes. However, under the current Control of Pesticides Regulations, professional products can only be used by persons with a certificate of competence recognized by Ministers. Unless, that is, one was born prior to nineteen-sixty-four and is using the product on one's own or one's employer's land."

"That's interesting," Powell said offhandedly. Sir Reggie, bless his heart, had obviously been doing his homework. "How much of this Fluorobane would you need?"

"Three hundred milligrams of fluoroacetamide would be enough. It comes in hundred-gram sachets, so let's see . . . At three percent by weight of active ingredient you'd want to use ten grams of the bait—a couple of good spoonfuls would do the trick." The pathologist leaned back in his chair and eyed Powell speculatively. "You realize, of course, that there is a much simpler explanation for all of this: The poor bugger had the bad luck to get bitten by an adder and died as a result of complications related to some constitutional weakness, aggravated perhaps by the depressant effect of alcohol. It's not beyond the realm of possibility. That business about the pesticide shed could be just a coincidence."

Powell thought about this for a moment. "Simpler but less satisfying," he said eventually. "I have a feeling about this one, Reggie. Somebody murdered Dinsdale, I'm convinced of it. Whoever did it is extremely clever and thinks he got away with it." He looked at the pathologist, his eyes feverishly bright. "I don't know how or why it was done, but I'm bloody well going to find out."

CHAPTER 16

The next morning dawned ambiguously gray and Powell attempted once again to contact Chloe Aldershot without success. He then rang Sarah Evans before they left for the rail station and arranged to have her pick them up in Malton. An hour later, they were all driving together back to Brackendale.

Powell asked Sarah how she had made out with her list. Although she'd been acting rather subdued after being introduced to Sir Reggie, he had the impression that she was fairly bursting with news.

"I managed to track down our missing farmer, Albert Turner. He got home yesterday morning, rather the worse for the wear and tear. He'd been off drinking with his mates in Goathland apparently. His wife called me in the afternoon to tell me—after she'd had a chance to deal with him, I expect. I drove up to their farm to interview him and—"

Sir Reggie began to snore loudly in the backseat.

Powell grinned. "Don't mind him—he had a late night."

"Right." She looked relieved. "Anyway, we had a very interesting chat. It seems that he's on the verge of losing his farm. According to Mr. Turner, the price of sheep is down and the costs keep going up. He claims that the estate raising his rent this year was the last straw."

"I got much the same story from Katie Elger," Powell observed.

"Not surprisingly, Turner seems to be using his financial troubles as an excuse for his drinking. The thing is . . ." Sarah paused significantly. "I got the impression that he blamed Dickie Dinsdale for his problems—in a personal way, I mean."

Powell sighed. "Why am I not surprised? What did he have to say about the events of the farmers' shoot?"

She shrugged. "Same as the others. Claims he didn't hear or see a thing."

"Did you manage to track down that other chap and his son?"

"Brian Whyte. Same story. He and his son, Tony—" She stopped and wrinkled her nose. She glanced at Powell.

A look of alarm crossed his face as he turned to watch Sir Reggie snorting and rumbling in the backseat. He quickly rolled down the window. "We, er, went out for Indian last night," he said sheepishly.

They looked at each other and began to laugh at the same time.

"Well, at least we know he's human," she quipped.

Powell reached for his cigarettes. "You won't mind if I smoke, then?"

"I assume that's a rhetorical question."

Powell lit a cigarette and inhaled deeply. "Carry on with your report, Evans."

"Right. Basically, the accounts of what happened that afternoon are all consistent. Not one of them appears to have noted anything out of the ordinary while they waited in their shooting butts for the fog to lift. I've talked with the other beaters, as well, and it's the same story."

"What we have, then," Powell mused aloud, "is a scenario where any one of the fifteen individuals involved in the shoot—let's exclude Dinsdale for the moment—could have been wandering about all over the moor doing as they bloody well pleased without being seen for at least half an hour. Does that about sum it up?"

Sarah hesitated. "I suppose."

"And furthermore, most of them are probably glad to see Dinsdale dead."

"That's a bit unfair, isn't it?"

"Is it? By the way, did you get a chance to talk to Francesca, the maid?"

She shook her head. "She's next on my list."

"Anything more on Felicity?"

"It seems she does have a bit of a reputation for, er, playing the field. But the word is she's got a steady now."

"Really?"

"You'll never guess who it is."

"Please tell me, Evans."

"Mick Curtis."

This caught Powell's attention. "It looks like our Mick's an ambitious lad," he said slowly.

"Perhaps they're in love," Sarah rejoined.

Powell looked at her. "Do you have anything else?"

She was a bit taken aback by her superior's cool formality. "Yes, sir. You wanted to know what was on the lunch menu for the farmers' shoot. Mrs. Settle's veal-and-ham pie with peach crumble for afters."

Powell found himself contemplating the possibility of a freshly baked peach crumble with an oatmeal topping liberally sprinkled with Fluorobane. Or a glass of claret laced with sodium cyanide. He shared his thoughts with his detective-sergeant. "Somebody poisoned him, Evans. I can feel it in my bones."

She swallowed. "There's something else you should know, then. Guess who made the dessert?"

Powell sighed. "In case you haven't guessed by now, Evans, I don't like guessing games."

"Yes, sir. Well, according to Mrs. Settle, our landlady, Mrs. Walker, brought the crumble, as well as the wine."

"Really? How *is* Mrs. Walker, by the way?"

"Still in bed with her migraine, as far as I know."

Powell stared out the window at the passing fields. "We'll have to see about that."

They stopped briefly in Pickering to see Dr. Harvey. He and Sir Reggie greeted each other like long-lost friends, having met before at a conference dealing with the finer points of cutting up cadavers or whatever pathologists talk about when they get together. Harvey had contacted the Forensic Science Service at the Wetherby Home Office earlier that morning and was able to confirm that the results of the toxicological analyses would be available the next day.

When they got back to Brackendale, Powell suggested

to Sarah that she run up to East Moor with Sir Reggie to have a look at the grouse butts. The expression of dread on her face was almost comical. After they'd gone, he wandered over to the garage and learned that his car would be ready in about an hour. He went back to the inn and rang Sergeant Black at the Yard.

"I've got something for you, Mr. Powell."

"Shoot."

"I went to see John Newbury, Ronnie Dinsdale's solicitor, this morning. He was reluctant at first—gave me the usual song and dance about solicitor-client privilege—but when I explained that we were only interested in the gist of Dinsdale's will, he agreed to cooperate. It seems that Dinsdale has willed his entire estate to his son, Richard, with the exception of a sum of money that goes to his wife, Marjorie. Newbury refused to say how much, but I get the impression we're talking about a few hundred thousand pounds. In the event that Dinsdale was predeceased by his son, the wife gets the whole lot."

"Is that so?"

"I thought you'd be interested, sir."

"Did you ask him about the Hull Water Corporation scheme?"

"He was a bit cagey, but I got the feeling he knows something about it."

"Anything else?

"Well, sir, Mr. Newbury did give the impression that Dickie had been a great disappointment to his father. Marjorie, on the other hand, is apparently the light of old Dinsdale's life. A few years ago, he'd talked about changing his will, but never got around to it."

"I appreciate this, Bill."

Detective-Sergeant Black chuckled. "You can send me a postcard, sir."

"Any news on the commissioner's job?" Powell asked, as if by way of an afterthought.

"Not a bloody word, sir. It's pretty tense around here, as you can imagine."

"Well, keep your chin up, " Powell replied with unconvincing heartiness.

In the kitchen at Blackamoor Hall, Francesca Aguirre was cleaning up the mess she'd made. The bottle had slipped from her fingers and exploded like a bomb on the floor, splattering red wine everywhere. It looked just like blood, she thought morbidly. She leaned on the handle of her mop for a moment, brushing her long black hair from her eyes. She wondered how it had all gone so wrong. When she and her husband, Luis, had come to England a little more than two years ago, it had seemed like a wonderful dream, the chance to start a new life in a prosperous land of opportunity. But how quickly the dream had shattered in this cold English house on these black moors, just like the bottle she kept hidden away in the cupboard to dull her guilt and shame. She felt her stomach knot—she'd have to go down to the cellar to get another one now. She fingered the tiny gold crucifix hanging on a chain around her neck. She thought again about the enormity of what she had done. If Luis ever found out—

She whirled around suddenly, sending the mop clattering to the floor. "You! What do you want?"

Mick Curtis was standing in the doorway. "That's no

way to treat a fellow member of the working class. The help should stick together, don't you think?"

"Get out!" Her eyes blazed with hatred.

He sneered. "Don't flatter yourself, Francesca. I'm looking for Miss Jamieson. I thought she might be downstairs."

After he'd gone, she could not stop trembling. Eventually she went back to her work, scrubbing desperately at the stained flagstones.

The motor turned over first try and then rumbled happily. "Good as new, Mr. Powell," the mechanic pronounced.

Powell thanked him and backed the Triumph out of the garage. He got out and put up the top and a few minutes later he was heading north out of the village. With Sarah and Sir Reggie otherwise occupied, he had some time on his hands and decided that he had better have another word with Katie Elger. As he drove alongside the beck he reflected on his conversation with Bill Black. Marjorie Dinsdale was the major beneficiary of Dickie Dinsdale's death. By inheriting Blackamoor, she would be able to maintain the lifestyle to which she and her daughter had become accustomed. From all accounts, Ronnie Dinsdale's health was in a precarious state—had he died before Dickie, Marjorie would have been left with very little relative to the size of the estate. She and Felicity possibly would have had to leave Blackamoor Hall. And there was something else, something perhaps more important to her than money. Powell had come away with a strong impression of Mrs. Dinsdale's fierce loyalty to her husband, her sense of pride in his reputation both as a businessman and as landlord to the residents of Brackendale. A legacy that was threatened by her stepson's exploits . . . Did she know for instance that Dickie was a Peeping Tom who got his kicks by spying on her daughter?

It was in this pensive state of mind that Powell took the turn into Dale End Farm. The high tops were obscured now by clouds and a gusty wind was driving dark streaks of rain across the head of the dale. The first drops splattered the windscreen as he pulled up in front of the house.

CHAPTER 17

Katie Elger answered the door with a look of surprise. "Come in, Chief Superintendent."

Powell smiled. "I've had some work done on my car and I was just out for a test drive. Is your father in?"

A flicker of concern in her expression. "No. Why do you ask?"

"I was hoping to meet him."

"He's gone to Helmsley," she explained as she led him into the kitchen. "The National Park Authority offers grant aid to farmers to help them conserve traditional features on their land, such as drystone walls and historic buildings. There's an old barn on the farm that Dad would like to restore. He's gone to see about it."

Powell settled himself at the table. "I'll get right to the point, Katie. I believe that Dickie Dinsdale was murdered. Furthermore, I think the key to the whole thing lies in the sequence of events that began in the shooting box and ended in his death in the grouse butt on East Moor."

Her blue eyes probed his. "I don't understand—the adder—I mean, how could it be murder?"

"I think he was poisoned. There are two possibilities: the snakebite was either an incredible coincidence or a brilliant ruse. I haven't yet decided which."

Katie shook her head numbly. "I still don't understand."

"If Dinsdale *was* poisoned, I'm trying to determine who had the opportunity. So I'd like you to tell me again exactly what happened that afternoon, sparing no detail, however trivial it might seem. You told me before that you were helping Mrs. Settle with lunch in the shooting box. Was anyone else helping you?"

"Emma Walker brought the dessert and gave us a hand with the serving."

"It was a peach crumble, I understand."

Katie tossed him a curious look. "That's right."

"Katie, I'd like you to think very carefully about this before you answer. Is there any possible way that somebody could have poisoned Dinsdale at lunch? The most likely poisons are a granular rat bait that looks a bit like cereal or a white soluble powder."

She frowned thoughtfully. "I remember that he arrived late—we'd already started serving the men. Mrs. Settle's veal-and-ham pie was the main course, followed by the crumble. Wine was served with the meal and a glass of port afterward." She hesitated. "It's possible, I suppose. I mean, somebody could have sprinkled the rat bait over Dickie's crumble. It wouldn't have looked too out of place with cream poured over it, I shouldn't think. The other possibility would have been to doctor his drink with your soluble powder. The problem is," she said in a flat voice, "almost anyone could have done it." She looked at him. "Including me."

He smiled thinly. "How so?"

"Well, Mrs. Settle, Emma Walker, and I were doing most of the serving, but several others pitched in as well. I can't remember who did what, specifically, but there were eighteen or nineteen people in the shooting box, so it was pretty chaotic."

"Try to think, Katie. Can you remember anyone else besides the three of you serving food or drink to Dinsdale?"

"No, I'm sorry."

Powell was disappointed. "Right. Do you recall what time lunch began and ended?"

"I think it was around noon when we started serving. I remember it was just after two o'clock when I set out for the butts after helping Mrs. Settle with the washing up, so we must have finished lunch about half an hour earlier."

"Was Emma Walker still there?"

Katie shook her head. "She only stayed a few minutes."

"How would you describe Dinsdale's demeanor during lunch?"

Her manner stiffened. "Same as always, you could say."

"Could you be a little more specific?"

Her eyes flashed angrily. "He was behaving like a drunken boor. Is that specific enough?"

"Did he appear unwell in any way?"

"Not so as you'd know it."

"Did anybody else appear to behave oddly?"

"I'd say everyone was having a pretty good time, Chief Superintendent. Even Dinsdale being there couldn't put a damper on—" She stopped suddenly, an odd expression on her face.

"What is it, Katie?"

"I remember now that Emma Walker seemed quite upset about something, but I suppose that's not surprising considering what Dinsdale did to her parents."

"Did she say anything?"

"Not to me."

"You said you left the shooting box around two. What was your intention?"

"It was miserable out. I was taking my father a flask of tea."

"So you set out for the butts."

"Yes."

"You're aware that your father had decided not to shoot and was out on the moor with the other beaters?"

"I didn't know that at the time."

"All right, Katie, I want you to tell me again exactly what happened after you set out from the shooting box. Please don't leave anything out."

In a calm tone of voice, she once again described her chilling experience: becoming disoriented in the fog, hearing the two shots, then seeing Mick Curtis standing white as a ghost beside the butt; bending down over Dinsdale and seeing the adder writhing in its death throes beside him. "I still dream about it," she said matter-of-factly.

Powell nodded. "Thank you, Katie. You've been most helpful. I imagine you'll be starting university again soon," he added casually.

She grimaced. "Classes start next week. I'll be moving back to college on the weekend."

"Biology, isn't it?"

She nodded.

"I was talking to a graduate student in biology at York just yesterday."

"Oh, yes?"

"Stumpy Macfarlane. You must know him."

She hesitated for an instant. "I've heard of him, of course."

"I thought you might have run into him at the university."

She blushed, clearly flustered now. "Did you say he was a graduate student?"

"You do know him, don't you, Katie?"

"I know all about his run-in with Dinsdale and the police on the grouse moor, but I didn't know him then . . ." She lapsed awkwardly into silence.

"It would be best if you told me about it."

She sighed. "Why does everything have to be so complicated?"

He smiled thinly. "I only know that it's simpler in the long run to tell the truth."

She met his gaze, a hint of defiance in her eyes. "I suppose you're right. After all, we've got nothing to hide. Yes, I know Michael. He gave a lecture in York at the end of August on the environmental issues facing this country. I stayed at the end to tell him that I disagreed with the tactics he'd used against Dinsdale, which is bloody something coming from me. Don't get me wrong, shooting birds for sport or watching a pack of frenzied dogs tear apart a fox is not my idea of enlightened resource management, but I do resent outsiders coming in and telling people how to live their lives. If attitudes towards blood sports are to change, evolution has to occur within the rural community. And the fact remains that a lot of country folk still rely on traditional pursuits for part of their income."

"From what I know of Stumpy, er, Michael, it must have been an interesting discussion," Powell observed dryly.

"I was simply making the point that farmers like my father are conservationists as well. Dad has farmed this land for forty years and he's put back much more than he's taken. He's painstakingly restored derelict hedgerows and rebuilt drystone walls. He's fenced off woodlands to promote wildlife. He doesn't overgraze or use herbicides on his flower meadows. He's planted saplings to ensure trees for the future—I could go on and on. The point is, environmentalists would do well to regard traditional farmers as allies in their cause rather than adversaries."

"You have me convinced. What about Michael?"

"I think Michael has come to the realization that he can't spend the rest of his life lying down in front of bulldozers. He'd already decided to do a graduate degree in biology when we met, and I've had him out here to look at the farm. He seems to be impressed."

Listening to her, Powell couldn't help but be impressed himself. "I can see why he would be," he said. But was she being entirely forthright? "There's just one more thing, Katie. What do you know about this Hull Water Corporation business?"

"Michael told me about it."

"Before it hit the newspapers?"

She nodded.

"Do you know how he found out about it?"

"I know all about Chloe Aldershot, if that's what you mean. It's over between Michael and her—that's all I care about."

"I imagine you know that the protest on Dinsdale's grouse moor had nothing to do with cruelty to animals but was intended as a warning to Dinsdale to back off on the water scheme?"

"Dinsdale was willing to put half of Brackendale, including this farm, under thirty feet of water simply to line his own pockets!" Katie said fiercely. "When Michael explained the real reason for the protest, I understood why he had to do it."

Powell persisted. "Michael told me that he had plans to escalate the campaign, to do whatever it took to stop Dinsdale. Do you have any idea what he had in mind?"

"Are you asking me if he intended to kill Dickie?" she asked indignantly.

Powell didn't think a reply was necessary.

The young woman shook her head stubbornly. "If you really knew Michael, you'd realize how absurd the suggestion is. "

Powell got to his feet. "Does your father know about you and Michael?"

She looked slightly uncomfortable. "I haven't found a way to tell him yet."

As Powell drove back to the village through a steady drizzle, he couldn't help wondering what Lord Aldershot's elusive daughter, Chloe the aristocratic anarchist, thought about Stumpy turning all respectable and falling for a farmer's daughter.

*   *   *

That evening, Powell, Sarah Evans, and Sir Reggie drove into Kirkbymoorside for dinner. Later, cozily ensconced in the bar of the King's Crown, a former seventeenth-century coaching inn presided over by a charming landlord who looked like Inspector Morse, they got down to comparing notes. Or rather Powell and Sarah compared notes. Sir Reggie—who, at irregular intervals and without any hint of a warning, sneezed explosively, causing his companions and the other unsuspecting patrons to jump—was sulking. His large red face was even redder than usual and he snuffled noisily into a damp handkerchief. "Damned weather in these parts," he muttered.

Sarah seemed worried that Sir Reggie held her responsible for his present state. "We could have caught our death up on that moor," she agreed with the pathologist.

"Nonsense, exposure to the elements is the best restorative for the soul," Powell rejoined.

An ominous rumble from Sir Reggie.

She glared at Powell. "After we located Dinsdale's shooting butt, we undertook a *thorough* inspection," she said, obviously making a point.

"Don't know how anyone could have missed it," Sir Reggie grumbled.

"Missed what?" Powell asked, in spite of himself.

"A loose stone in the front wall of the butt about a foot above the ground," Sarah said. "When you slide it out, there's a sort of cavity in the wall, extending back perhaps two feet."

"This is interesting, Evans. Tell me more."

"With the stone in place, the size of the cavity would

be about a foot wide, six inches high, and a foot and a half deep." She paused to let this sink in. "Just about big enough for an adder to squeeze into, I expect."

"That's just what I was thinking," Powell said.

"There's more," Sir Reggie interjected gruffly. "On the inside walls of this little grotto, I noticed a few small dark stains. Could be blood."

"I've got the scene-of-crime team coming out from Pickering tomorrow to check it out," Sarah added.

"Brilliant work, you two," Powell pronounced. "This calls for another drink, I think." He went up to the bar and returned with a pint for himself, a hot buttered rum for Sir Reggie, and a tonic-and-lime for Sarah, who had volunteered to be their designated driver for the evening.

"Let's say, just for the sake of argument," Powell mused aloud, "that our hypothetical murderer managed somehow to capture an adder and keep it imprisoned in the wall of the butt until the day of the farmers' shoot. At some point during the proceedings, he or she slips some poison to Dinsdale; when he collapses in his butt, the villain lets the snake out to nip poor Dickie as a diversionary tactic." He looked questioningly at Sarah.

"Or perhaps he forced Dinsdale's hand into the hole in the wall where the snake was? That would explain the bloodstains," Sarah suggested.

Sir Reggie sniffed indignantly. "I think this is all highly speculative and furthermore—" His face suddenly turned an alarming shade of purple. "Ah-ah-*choo*!" he bellowed.

"Bless you," Powell and Sarah said in unison.

"When we get the results of the toxicological tests tomorrow," Sir Reggie continued as if nothing had happened, oblivious of the startled reaction his latest sternutation had caused in the bar, "we'll know for certain what we're dealing with." He looked first at Powell and then at Sarah. "The truth, as they say, is in the crumble."

CHAPTER 18

Powell and Detective-Sergeant Evans took advantage of the hiatus afforded by Sir Reggie's departure for the gents to continue down the same speculative road.

"Assuming that Dinsdale *was* in fact poisoned," Sarah ventured, "and assuming that the adder was part of the plan, how could the killer have known that Dinsdale would end up in the right butt? Don't they draw lots or something?"

"That's the normal drill. However, according to Harry Settle, it was no secret that Dinsdale preferred that particular butt because it generally provided the best shooting. And since there weren't any paying guests to offend, he evidently just commandeered it. We should confirm that with Mick Curtis, however."

Sarah frowned, obviously not satisfied. "I keep coming back to that damned snake. It just seems too clever by half. Why not just poison him and be done with it?"

Powell's reply was interrupted by the pathologist's clamorous return. Time to change gears, he decided. Sir

184

Reggie was right. Idle speculation was getting them nowhere fast. "Apart from showing up my shoddy detective work, did you manage to accomplish anything else today?" he asked.

Sarah nodded eagerly. "I managed to dig up some dirt on Mick Curtis."

Powell put down his glass, his interest piqued. "What do you mean?"

"After we finished up on the moor, we paid a visit to Blackamoor Hall. I wanted to have a word with Francesca Aguirre. I left Reggie in Mrs. Dinsdale's charge to dry off in front of the fire then—"

"Perfectly charming woman," Sir Reggie volunteered.

"Anyway, Francesca and I had an interesting chat. She was obviously upset about something and it was a bit of a struggle getting her to open up. She and her husband, Luis, have only been over here from Spain a couple of years," she added parenthetically. "To make a long story short, it seems that she and Mick Curtis had a relationship."

"A relationship?"

"Well, sort of. I mean, on one occasion, anyway."

Powell affected an air of shocked amazement. "You mean he shagged her in the scullery?"

"You could put it that way," she said frostily.

"Why is this relevant, Evans?"

"Francesca claims that he took advantage of her."

"What do you mean, 'took advantage'?"

"Forced himself on her, like."

"Sexually assaulted her, you mean?"

"She implied as much but refused to go into details. They'd both been drinking, apparently."

"Come to the point, Evans," Powell said impatiently.

"The thing is, sir, according to Francesca, Curtis threatened her, told her if she said anything to anyone, he'd accuse her of stealing and have her thrown in prison or deported or something. I think the poor woman is more afraid of her husband finding out and blaming *her* for what happened. Isn't it bloody typical?"

Powell sighed. "Spare me the speech, Evans. Is she willing to bring a complaint against him?"

"I wouldn't hold my breath."

Powell lapsed into silence. "I can't help wondering why she decided to tell someone about it now," he said eventually.

Sarah shrugged. "Maybe she just wanted to get it off her chest."

"Or maybe she wants to stick it to her former boyfriend for taking up with Felicity. But, giving her the benefit of the doubt, I can understand why Curtis, the fair-haired boy, would want to keep it from his employer."

"I don't imagine Felicity would be too thrilled about it either," she commented.

There was a sudden sonorous *clang* as the landlord struck a bell hanging over the bar. "Time, ladies and gentlemen!" he sang out.

Powell gulped down the last of his bitter. "It's probably a side issue," he concluded.

The next morning, Powell set out for Blackamoor Hall, leaving Sarah Evans and Sir Reggie behind to await the results of the toxicology tests. The sky was the color of gunmetal and hardly a breath of air stirred. As he climbed the steep incline of Blackamoor Bank Road through the thickening mist, he had the nagging sense that he was overlooking some small but crucial piece of evidence. He tried once again to sort out the Gordian knot of facts and speculation that threatened to bring his mental process to a grinding halt. Dickie Dinsdale, the unpopular heir to the Blackamoor estate, was found near death in his shooting butt during a grouse shoot, having been bitten by an adder. He died a short time later, but the precise cause of death remained unknown. It subsequently came to light that a shed where deadly pesticides are stored was broken into a few days before Dinsdale's death, raising the suspicion that he may have been poisoned.

If this was confirmed by the toxicological analysis, the next obvious question was, Who stood to benefit? His stepmother, Marjorie, came immediately to mind. With Dinsdale out of the way, she stood to inherit her husband's fortune, enabling her to maintain her lifestyle at Blackamoor Hall. One would have to include her daughter, Felicity, in the same category. However, it didn't appear that either of them had the opportunity—if Powell's idea of how the poisoning was carried out proved to be correct.

There were, of course, other potential motives for murder besides financial gain. Revenge, for instance. Harry Settle, the former head keeper, had a very large ax to grind—sacked, for all intents and purposes, after forty years of loyal service to the estate. Both he and his wife were present at the farmers' shoot. Mrs. Settle had been in charge of the meal at the shooting box and would undoubtedly have had an opportunity to slip something into Dinsdale's food or drink. And what about the Settles' daughter, the elusive Emma Walker? It was understandable that she would resent the way Dinsdale had treated her father. She, too, had been present at the shooting box and had even provided a dessert that was ideally suited to adulteration by one of the more deadly poisons stored in Harry Settle's shed.

The most intriguing possibility was that Dinsdale's death was related to the proposed scheme by the Hull Water Corporation to flood Brackendale for a reservoir. Dinsdale's negotiations with the company might well have remained secret if Stumpy Macfarlane had not been tipped off by his former girlfriend, Chloe Aldershot. After the events of August twelfth, there had obviously been no love lost between Macfarlane and Dinsdale, and Powell was convinced that Macfarlane was prepared to do whatever it took to stop the project. Powell sighed inwardly. He imagined that just about everyone in Brackendale had a stake in preventing Dinsdale doing a deal with the water company, including the beaters and the other guns who were on the moor that afternoon while Dinsdale lay dying in his shooting butt. Dinsdale had recently raised the rents, causing hardship for tenant farmers such as Frank Elger and Albert Turner—a tactic that was intended, Powell now surmised, to force them off their farms so that the landlord wouldn't have to buy out their leases before selling the land to the water company.

As the little Triumph climbed onto Blackamoor Rigg, Powell switched on the windscreen wipers as if to sweep away the clutter from his mind. The moor was completely obliterated by fog and he could barely make out the narrow swath of road illuminated by his headlamps. Off to his left, a dark shape suddenly loomed. He slowed the car to a crawl and turned into the graveled drive.

The massive oak door opened to reveal the forlorn figure of Francesca Aguirre. Her face was unnaturally pale and devoid of any expression or emotion, like the brittle image of someone long forgotten in a faded, sepia photograph.

"Is Mrs. Dinsdale in?" Powell inquired.

Francesca shook her head. "She's taken Mr. Dinsdale to see the doctor."

"How about Ms. Felicity?"

She averted her eyes and stepped aside.

Felicity was in the sitting room, still in her dressing gown, flipping through a fashion magazine. She looked up as Powell entered the room. "Chief Superintendent, this is a surprise." She crossed her long legs and smiled. "I must look a fright."

"I apologize for barging in unannounced like this, but I was wondering if I might ask you a few more questions?"

She affected an expression of mock concern. "It sounds serious. You'd better sit down."

"Felicity, I have reason to believe that your stepbrother was murdered," he said solemnly.

There was no visible reaction. "What's it got to do with me?"

How touching. "I'd like to take you back to September thirteenth, the day your stepbrother died," he began. "As I understand it, the farmers' shoot got going in the morning, but Dickie didn't turn up at the shooting box until around noon. Do you have any idea where he was?"

She appeared to give the question some thought. "I'm afraid I can't help you," she said.

A somewhat ambiguous answer, Powell thought. He tried again. "Do you remember seeing him at all that morning?"

"I can hardly remember what happened yesterday, let alone two weeks ago. Now that I think about it, I think he might have gone into the village that morning. Maybe you should ask Mummy?"

"I'll do that. By the way, what do you think of this resort scheme your stepbrother was promoting?"

She shrugged. "At least it would have livened up the bloody place."

"I see. I won't take up much more of your time, Felicity, but there is one more thing . . ."

"Yes?"

"I understand that you've been seeing Mick Curtis?"

She looked at him, her blue eyes cool and appraising. "I think that's between me and Mick, don't you?"

Powell didn't answer.

She sighed. "After the protest. Mick started coming round the Hall more and, well, one thing led to another."

"Did Dickie know about your relationship?"

"You make it sound so serious. Look, Chief Superintendent, Mick is extremely good looking and he amuses me. That's all there is to it."

He didn't believe her somehow. "Does Mick feel the same way?"

"You'd have to ask him about that."

"You didn't answer my original question, Felicity. Did Dickie know about you and Mick?"

"Like I told you before, he got off on prying into my personal affairs."

"What do you mean exactly?"

"Whenever I took my boyfriends up to my room at night, Dickie would listen at the door, and I'd try to catch the little wanker in the act. It was a little game we played."

"Was Mick involved in this game, as you put it?"

She smiled without humor. "It's not like I told him my perverted stepbrother was going to listen in while we were doing it. Anyway, Dickie must have recognized Mick's voice one night. He was absolutely furious. I think it was the idea of his stepsister being screwed by a member of the working class that bothered him." She smiled bitterly. "It must have upset his sense of social order. He certainly didn't give a damn about me."

"Did Dickie say anything to Mick?"

Her sudden laughter struck a harsh note. "Dickie always considered his own interests above everything else. He'd just sacked one head keeper; he couldn't afford to lose another one with the shooting season just starting. But he told me that he was going to get rid of Mick at the end of the season. I tried to reason with him, but it was useless."

"When did this happen?"

"I can't remember exactly—around the end of August, I think."

"And Mick didn't know anything about it?"

She shook her head.

"Why didn't you tell him?"

"It would've upset him, wouldn't it? Besides, I still hoped that Dickie would change his mind."

"Does your mother know about any of this?"

"I don't discuss my love life with my mother, Chief Superintendent. Do you with yours?"

"I'm afraid she'd be bored to tears. Are you and Mick still seeing each other?"

She frowned. "Mick hasn't been himself since Dickie died. It really hit him hard. I think he just needs some time."

Despite what she'd said previously, it sounded like Mick was more than just her boy toy. What was it that Rashid had said about love that day in the restaurant?

CHAPTER 19

As he drove into the village, his mobile phone began to beep insistently. He fumbled for it in his jacket pocket as he pulled over to the side of the road. "Powell."

"It's Evans, sir. We just got the results of the blood tests back. We're with Dr. Harvey now." There was the muffled sound of conversation in the background. She paused as if drawing a deep breath. "Dinsdale died from cyanide poisoning; there's no question about it."

It seemed almost anticlimactic. "What about the flask?"

"Nothing except whisky."

"Well, this is it," Powell said. "Is Reggie handy?"

"Hold on."

A few seconds later he heard the pathologist grumbling on the other end. "Reggie," Powell said, "is there any way that sodium cyanide could take as long as two hours, or even longer, to act?"

Sir Reggie launched into a discussion on the factors affecting the rate of decomposition of the sodium salt into hydrocyanic acid in the stomach. He conceded that it would be somewhat unusual for that amount of time to transpire before a lethal dose of sodium cyanide took effect, but it wasn't impossible.

"So Dinsdale could have been poisoned before he arrived at the shooting box. He got there sometime after twelve and was found in his butt around two-thirty."

Sir Reggie grunted in a noncommittal fashion. "If he had a full stomach or achlorhydria—"

"What's that?" Powell interrupted.

"An absence of stomach acid secretions. It occurs in about one in twenty normal people without causing symptoms. A reduced concentration of hydrochloric acid in the stomach would tend to retard the release of hydrocyanic acid."

Powell thought about this for a moment. "What if he'd taken some bicarb?"

"An antacid, taken in large enough quantity, would have a similar effect, although it would only be temporary."

"Thanks, Reggie. Put Sarah back on again, would you?"

Powell gathered his thoughts for a moment. "Sarah, I'd like you to track down Stumpy's ex-girlfriend, Chloe Aldershot . . ." He flipped open his notebook and recited the telephone number. "If necessary, run over to York and interview her. I want to know how tight Stumpy's alibi is. I wouldn't be at all surprised if she weren't just a little disappointed in her old comrade." In answer to her question, he explained about Stumpy and Katie Elger. "I'm heading back to the inn to see if I can raise Mrs. Walker from her sickbed. I'll see you later." He disconnected abruptly.

* * *

He found Robert Walker alone in the pub. The landlord looked up from his newspaper. "Morning, Chief Superintendent. What'll it be?"

"I'd kill for a cup of coffee."

He smiled. "No problem. I've got a pot on in the kitchen. White or black?"

"White, please." Walker folded his newspaper and went to fetch it. He returned a few minutes later with a steaming mug of coffee. He produced a bowl of sugar and a spoon from behind the bar and set them in front of Powell. "How's the investigation going?" he asked casually.

"We're making headway," Powell replied. "As a matter of fact, we've just confirmed this morning that Dickie Dinsdale was poisoned. We think it was a type of rat poison containing sodium cyanide."

"You mean an accident, like," Walker said slowly.

Powell stared at him. "Not an accident, Mr. Walker. Cold-blooded murder."

"Murder? I don't understand."

"It appears that he was poisoned a short time before being found in his shooting butt."

"But the adder . . ."

"If Dinsdale was killed by a snake, Mr. Walker, it was the two-legged variety."

Walker swallowed hard but said nothing.

"I understand that your wife helped prepare the lunch that day."

Walker stared blankly at him.

"She provided the dessert for the occasion," Powell prompted. "A peach crumble, I believe."

The landlord shrugged stiffly. "She helps her mum out every year."

"How are Mr. and Mrs. Settle, by the way?"

"All right. We'll be helping them move into their flat in Scarborough on the weekend."

"I imagine it'll be quite a change for them."

"You could say that," Walker said in a flat voice.

"I take it Mrs. Walker is feeling better, then?"

He wiped the bar with a towel. "Still under the weather, I'm afraid. Her migraines often last a week or more."

"I thought you said she'd be helping you move her parents on the weekend?"

"Well, I meant only if she feels up to it."

"Would you tell Mrs. Walker I'd like to have a word with her? When she's feeling better."

"What is it you want to ask her?" he asked. "Maybe I can help?"

Powell sipped his coffee. "It can wait. But there is something you might be able to help me with. I've been informed that Dinsdale was in the village that morning. You didn't happen to see him, did you?"

"What's this all about?" Walker asked, his manner defensive.

"It's strictly routine, Mr. Walker. I'm simply trying to trace his movements in the hours leading up to his death."

Walker did not respond immediately, as if he were weighing his options. "Yeah, I saw him," he said eventually.

"Where?"

"Here, at the inn."

"Do you remember approximately what time it would have been?"

"It was just before opening time, around ten-thirty, I think."

"Did he just drop in out of the blue?"

"No," the landlord admitted grudgingly. "I'd called him up the day before. Told him I wanted to talk to him."

"Go on."

Walker's face flushed. "About the bloody reservoir. I tried to get him to understand the impact it would have on the lives of everyone who lived in the dale. But the bastard just laughed at me. I shouldn't have expected anything else, I suppose, after the way he'd treated Harry."

"So you did know about the water scheme at that point."

He nodded. "There had been rumors flying about ever since that protest on Dinsdale's grouse moor."

Strategically leaked by Stumpy, Powell had little doubt. "Can you be a bit more specific about the nature of your conversation?"

Walker's expression darkened. "Dindsale stated his view that the only people who might be negatively affected by the sort of 'progress' he envisioned for Brackendale were a few marginal farmers and a handful of small businessmen in the village, like myself. All expendable, as far as he was concerned, with token compensation."

"I see. Was Mrs. Walker present during your meeting with Dinsdale?"

"She was in and out, as I recall. She was getting ready for the farmers' shoot lunch."

"I heard that she appeared to be upset about something when she was at the shooting box."

"That's understandable, don't you think?"

"Perhaps. Tell me, Mr. Walker, did you serve Dinsdale a drink when he was here that morning?"

The landlord's eyes narrowed. "What are you getting at?"

"Just answer the question," Powell said, an edge to his voice.

"Yes, I served him a bloody drink."

"What was it?"

"How do you expect me to remember that?"

"I've got all day."

Walker sighed. "He liked malt whisky and French wine. It would have been one or the other." He hesitated. "Look, Chief Superintendent, I'll save you a lot of time and bother. I hated Dickie Dinsdale's guts, but I can assure you that I didn't kill him."

Powell drained his coffee cup. "I'm happy to hear that, Mr. Walker."

Powell went up to his room and rang Sarah Evans on her mobile phone. She was on her way to York with Sir Reggie to interview Chloe Aldershot. He arranged to meet her in Kirkbymoorside on her way back. After his little chat with Robert Walker, he wasn't sure that the atmosphere in the Lion and Hippo would be conducive to an evening of relaxed conversation.

Around four o'clock, Sarah called to let him know that she was just coming into Malton. She also informed him that she had put Sir Reggie, who was still in a snit, on a train back to London. When Powell left the inn, one side of the dale was illuminated by the afternoon sun, the other was immersed in deepening shadow. Powell drove into Kirkbymoorside with his mind in neutral and parked in front of the King's Crown. He decided on a stroll around the Market Place to kill time.

The hotel was located near the top of the High Market Place next door to the house where the second Duke of Buckingham, the notorious George Villiers, supposedly died after a hunting accident in 1687. He strolled past the news agent and the post office, two more historic hotels, and then a row of tidy redbrick semidetached houses with doors and window trim painted bright blue and green and navy. He crossed the road and browsed at the garden center for a few minutes before heading back towards the King's Crown. The Market Place was nearly deserted now, but once a week market stalls line the street, as they have done every Wednesday for six hundred years, and the town bustles with a traditional market. He passed St. Chads and the Methodist church and stopped for a moment to peer in the window of a Chinese restaurant that was sandwiched like a red-and-cream pagoda between two larger buildings.

He detoured into Church Street to investigate a queue of people spilling out of a doorway next to yet another pub. It was a tiny fish-and-chip shop packed with customers stopping in on the way home to pick up their suppers. Through the steamy window, Powell could see the staff serving up impressive slabs of battered fish and mountains of chips. He stood there for a moment, the smell of hot fat and vinegar having triggered an inexplicable wave of nostalgia. As he turned to leave, he nearly collided with a small gray-haired lady in a wool coat and wool hat, clutching her grease-stained package.

She looked up and smiled at him. "You should try

some, luv. They're not as greasy as some of the others. I have to be careful these days—too much fat doesn't agree with my chemo—but I always say if you can't enjoy yourself now and then, there's not much point, is there?"

He smiled. "I think, madame, you have discovered the secret of a happy life."

She beamed at him. "Bye-bye, luv." Such a nice young man, she thought, as she hurried home to her cat.

CHAPTER 20

"Well, let's have it," Powell said, setting his half-empty glass down on the table in front of him.

"Well, our Chloe's quite a girl," Sarah began. "Twenty years old and the only daughter of Lord Aldershot, former advisor to Lady Thatcher on northern issues. The old boy owns half of Yorkshire, from what I can gather. Anyway, a year or so ago she decided to chuck the whole thing—you know, Royal Ascot, the endless parties, the weekends in London dancing the night away at the Ministry of Sound—"

"I get the point, Evans."

"Yes, sir. Like I was saying, she decided to give up the frivolous life of a deb and devote herself instead to saving the world. She enrolled at the University of York last year, which is where she met Stumpy. They began a relationship that ended just a couple weeks ago, according to Chloe."

"Did she seem upset about it?"

"Not so's you'd notice. She seemed more disappointed than anything."

"What do you mean?"

"Well, it's like you said. I think she reckons Stumpy has sold out. Apparently he told her he wants to become an organic farmer when he finishes his degree."

"Does she know about Katie Elger?"

Sarah shrugged. "If she does, she didn't mention it." She hesitated. "It's hard to explain, but I got the impression that their relationship was more ideological than romantic."

"They must have had some jolly times together," Powell remarked sarcastically.

Sarah ignored his comment. "Just before she moved into residence this summer," she went on, "Chloe was at her parents' home in Richmond, collecting her things, when she overheard her father talking to someone on the telephone about the Hull Water Corporation proposal for Brackendale. Lord Aldershot is one of the principals of the company," she added by way of explanation. "Chloe confronted him and threatened to go to the press. He denied the whole affair, told her to get out, and more or less disowned her on the spot. She decided at that moment to do whatever she had to do to stop the project. It was shortly after that, that she recruited Stumpy to the cause."

"Before you continue, I'd be interested to hear your thoughts on her motivation."

Sarah thought for a moment. "There's no doubt she thinks it's wrong to destroy one of the most scenic dales in the country for profit—what rational person wouldn't?—

but I also think that, for whatever reason, she's trying to get back at her father."

Powell nodded. "Go on."

"They planned the August twelfth protest together, hoping to scare Dinsdale off. Stumpy was incensed with Dinsdale and the local police over the way he was treated and began to make plans with Chloe for the next phase of the campaign. She claims that she didn't see much of him after the end of August. His excuse was he needed to get organized for school as well as prepare for court—the case against Stumpy, Chloe, and the other protesters will be heard on October 11 and Stumpy's case against the police comes up sometime in early November. I don't know if she believed him, though."

"I think by then he'd shifted his attentions to Katie Elger," Powell commented.

"That may be, sir, but he hadn't cut the cord entirely. Chloe says he spent the night with her on September twelfth."

"Right. According to Inspector Braughton, she's his alibi for the thirteenth, the day Dinsdale was killed."

"Well, not exactly, sir."

"What do you mean?" Powell asked sharply.

Sarah leaned forward in her chair. "Well, sir. She says she spent the night with him, all right, but she now claims that he left around mid-morning."

"Time enough to get up to Brackendale."

"Exactly."

"Did he tell her where he was going?"

"She says not."

"This is interesting, Evans. You've managed to kill two grouse with one barrel, if I may coin a phrase."

"Sir?"

"Not only has she discredited Stumpy's alibi, she's blown her own as well. Tell me, Evans, did Chloe Aldershot strike you as the type of person who might take desperate measures to achieve her ends?"

Sarah frowned. "That's a difficult question. She impressed me as being a very committed young woman, but I don't know about murder."

"All right. But isn't it fair to say that she and Stumpy were both committed to stopping Dinsdale, and that she had recently become concerned about Stumpy's devotion to the cause?" He looked at her.

"Yes, I think that's true. But even if both of them had a theoretical motive for killing Dinsdale, I don't see how either had the opportunity."

Powell sighed. "There's no shortage of motives in this bloody case; when all is said and done, I think it does come down to who had the opportunity. The way I see it, we're dealing with two groups of people. Those who were present during lunch at the shooting box, but not up on the moor: Mrs. Settle, Katie Elger, and Emma Walker. And those who were in both places: the fifteen other guns and beaters—including Frank Elger, Albert Turner, Brian Whyte and his son, the rest of the farmers, as well as Harry Settle and Mick Curtis. Have I missed anyone?"

"I don't think so, but I would take issue with one of the names on your list."

"Who might that be?"

"Katie Elger."

"What do you mean?"

"Well, we know she was up on the moor just after Dinsdale was discovered by Mick Curtis. We only have her word for it that she wasn't up there earlier."

"During the time she says she was lost in the fog?"

Sarah nodded. "It took Sir Reggie and me about ten minutes to walk from the shooting box to Dinsdale's butt the other day, and Sir Reggie is no marathon man. Yet Katie Elger says it took her nearly half an hour."

Powell frowned. "She doesn't seem the type, somehow, but you have a point. We'd better put Katie on the second list then, which includes everybody I've already mentioned except Mrs. Settle and Emma Walker. Now, if Dinsdale was poisoned during lunch, any one of them could have done it. If he was slipped the cyanide on the moor, it must have been by someone on our second list. It seems less likely, given the time lag involved, but not impossible that he was poisoned before he arrived at the shooting box. In that case, we're looking at a third list."

"Which would include Mrs. Walker, who arrived just before lunch and left shortly after," Sarah pointed out.

"Right. We know she was at the Lion and Hippo when Dinsdale came to see her husband earlier that morning. And we shouldn't forget about Marjorie Dinsdale or her daughter."

Sarah stared at the tiny bubbles rising in her tonic water. "I keep coming back to that damned adder," she said, frustration evident in her voice. "If it's truly part of this thing, then the person we want must be on your first list, someone who was up on the moor. There is another possibility, I suppose: The murderer may have had an accomplice. Someone slips Dinsdale the cyanide at lunch, then his or her partner inflicts the snakebite in the shooting butt to cover their tracks."

Powell nodded absently. An interesting possibility, he acknowledged to himself. But something didn't fit and, once again, he couldn't put his finger on it. His head was spinning and not from too much bitter: love and hate environmental protest destruction and profit mongering rat poison sodium cyanide grouse crumble fog and venomous snakes . . . If he could only find the common denominator. He lit a cigarette and inhaled sharply.

Sarah interrupted his reverie. "I noticed when we came in that they have roast grouse on the menu tonight. I'd like to try it. Are you game?"

He smiled wryly. "It's probably about the closest I'm going to get to a grouse this season, so why not?"

The grouse and the cabernet sauvignon were both excellent, and as they sat sipping their coffees, Powell spoke. "I know we promised not to talk about the case over dinner, but something has been bothering me. It's Mick Curtis."

"What do you mean?"

"The way Katie Elger described him when she first saw him. Pale and frightened looking—white as a ghost was the way she put it. It was no doubt quite a shock to find his employer a victim, by all appearances, of a venomous snake. It's just that—I don't know—Curtis doesn't strike me as the squeamish type. I can't help wondering if he might have seen something else that might explain it."

Sarah laughed. "I'm sure there's even the odd gamekeeper who's afraid of the dark, sir."

"Very funny. In any case, I'm going to have another

chat with him tomorrow. And I'd like you to have one more go at Mrs. Settle. They're moving to Scarborough on the weekend, so we may not get another chance. Go over the whole thing again with her. Who served what to whom, who poured the wine, where Dinsdale was seated in relation to everybody else—you get the general idea."

Sarah sighed. "Right."

Powell regarded her with amusement. "You'll soon learn, if you haven't already, Evans, that ninety percent of this job is sheer bloody boredom punctuated with the occasional moment of satisfaction when you finally get something right. I want you to know that I will be putting in a good word for you, for what it's worth, on the off chance that you are masochistic enough to want to continue in this line of work."

"Thank you, sir." Sergeant bloody Dogsbody, at your service, she thought sourly.

Powell had difficulty sleeping that night. The customary night breeze had not materialized and the air in his room was oppressive. He'd forced open his window the minuscule few inches it would go, but to little effect since his landlord had seen fit to turn on the central heating system full blast. Simply to torment him, he had little doubt. He'd rung Marion earlier and now lay thinking about how much more they needed to say to each other and what a fool he'd been and a hundred other things besides. And every so often some isolated thought or fragment or image connected to the investigation would pop uninvited into his head. When he could stand it no longer, he threw off the duvet, turned onto his back and tried to lay still, staring into the darkness until he eventually slipped into unconsciousness. His dreams were populated with grinning adders and maniacal chemists concocting lethal cocktails on an endless plain of blasted heath.

CHAPTER 21

By the time Powell got downstairs it was after nine o'clock and the dining room was deserted. He went back up and knocked on Sarah's door, but there was no response. He assumed that she must have already left for the Settles'. Retracing his steps, he walked into the dining room and poured himself a cup of coffee from the carafe on the sideboard. He checked his watch. He'd already arranged the previous evening to meet Mick Curtis at ten o'clock up on East Moor. It didn't leave him much time for breakfast. With a grimace he helped himself to a small bowl of cereal.

As he was leaving the inn, he encountered a subdued-looking Mr. Walker in the front hall. "When Ms. Evans gets back, tell her I've gone up to East Moor, would you? I should be back by noon."

"Yes, Mr. Powell," the landlord mumbled.

Powell parked his car at the shooting box and followed the track up to the shooting butts. As he topped the final rise, the full glory of the North York Moors, awash in morning sunlight, was spread out before him. To his right, the green furrow of upper Rosedale ploughed deep into the heart of the moors, with red-roofed farmsteads dotted here and there and fields enclosed by stone walls stretching away until they met a thousand acres of hazy moorland once trodden by Bronze Age chieftains and medieval monks. The purple of the heather and the vivid green of grass and bracken had faded now, giving way to highlights of bronze and gold and red. To the west, the line of stone shooting butts marched down into Brackendale. Sunlight glinted off a Land Rover parked about halfway down the slope, and he could see a figure working beside it.

When he got there a few minutes later, Mick Curtis was leaning on his shovel beside a pile of what looked like coarse sand that had been dumped beside the track. "Grit for the grouse," he explained curtly. "You said you wanted to talk to me?"

Powell nodded somberly. "I'll try not to take up too much of your time, Mr. Curtis. I don't know if you've heard, but we're now treating Mr. Dinsdale's death as a murder. He was poisoned."

Curtis looked surprised. "Poisoned? With what?"

"Sodium cyanide. I understand that it's used on the estate for gassing rats."

The gamekeeper nodded. "Vermin get into the pheasant feed."

"Harry Settle told me that someone broke into the shed where the pesticides are kept."

"Right. Around the beginning of September, I think it was. We figured it was just some kids out to make trouble. Nothing seemed to be missing, so we didn't bother to report it to the police."

"You and Harry are the only people with keys?"

"As far as I know."

"Well, whoever broke in and took the stuff knew what they were doing. The symptoms of cyanide poisoning aren't that specific and it's easy enough to miss if you're not looking for it."

"I'm a bit puzzled, Chief Superintendent. What about the adder?"

"Dinsdale was bitten by an adder, all right, but that's not what killed him."

"But cyanide acts fairly quickly doesn't it? We were all with Mr. Dinsdale in the shooting box—I don't see how anybody could have given it to him at lunch."

"You have a point, assuming that's when he was poisoned."

"You mean it could have been done some time before that?"

"It's possible."

"Come to think of it, Mr. Dinsdale did arrive a bit late. He didn't say where he'd been, so maybe . . ." He left the rest unsaid.

"There's another possibility, of course. He might have been slipped the cyanide up here on the moor."

Curtis appeared to ponder this for a moment. "That's possible, I suppose. It was foggy enough that anyone could have visited Mr. Dinsdale's butt without being seen. But it doesn't make any sense does it?"

Curtis's analysis evoked Powell's interest. "What do you mean?" he asked.

"I can only assume from what you've said that the

crime was planned in advance. How could the murderer have known what the weather was going to be like? Without the cover of the fog, he'd run the risk that somebody would see what he was up to when he slipped Mr. Dinsdale the cyanide."

"I've asked myself the same question, Mr. Curtis. And the same problem rears its ugly head when we try to explain the snake."

"I'm not sure I follow you."

"I'm convinced that the snake was part of the killer's plan—a diversionary tactic—and not just a gruesome coincidence. But to administer the poison, wait for it to take effect, then somehow contrive to have the adder bite the victim, all without being seen—well, it beggars belief unless you factor in the fog. At least that's the way it appears on the face of it."

Curtis looked doubtful. "Maybe the snakebite *was* just a coincidence. Stranger things have happened."

"I wonder if you could tell me again exactly what you saw when you found Mr. Dinsdale in his butt that afternoon?"

Curtis frowned. "I've already told you . . ."

"Please bear with me."

The gamekeeper shrugged. "Like I told you before, he was lying on the ground, sort of curled up in a fetal position. Except his right arm was stretched out. The snake was in the corner of the butt, near his hand. Without even thinking, I put a couple of loads of bird shot into it. That's when Katie Elger turned up."

"That's what's got me puzzled, Mr. Curtis. You behaved perfectly normally, as one might expect a gamekeeper to do under the circumstances. I imagine you have to shoot quite a few predators in your line of work, and you reacted instinctively when you saw the adder. You raised your gun and fired. You've probably done the same sort of thing a hundred times before. But Katie Elger describes you as looking petrified—white as a sheet, or words to that effect. I keep asking myself why."

"I have this thing about snakes," he said, edgy now. "And Mr. Dinsdale was lying there, twitching and groaning. How would you expect me to look?" He absently rubbed the back of his right hand through his fingerless glove.

Powell was still not satisfied. "Perhaps you saw something else you haven't told me about."

Curtis seemed to relax slightly. "Look, Chief Superintendent, I've already told you what I saw."

Suddenly it hit him. Felicity had lied to him. Powell knew now who murdered Dickie Dinsdale. The why, the how, and the wherefore. At some level, he realized that he'd known all along. It was as if a dozen apparently unrelated facts simmering away in the ferment of his unconscious had suddenly boiled over into his conscious mind.

"Now, will there be anything else?" Curtis was asking, an element of impatience creeping into his voice. "I do have work to do."

Powell's eyes settled momentarily on the ridge behind the gamekeeper. He decided to take his chances. He looked at Curtis. "Why didn't you just say that the adder bit you when you tried to help your employer? It would have been so much simpler."

Curtis turned deathly pale. "Wh-what are you talking about?"

"You rigged it so you drew the butt next to Dinsdale's. After you got him settled in his shooting butt, you slipped him the poison. How did you do it, Mick? Did you offer him a dram of whisky laced with cyanide from your own flask?"

Curtis's face tightened. "Keep going, Chief Superintendent. This is starting to get interesting."

Powell smiled without humor. "I'll assume I'm on the right track, then. By the way, breaking into the pesticide shed to divert attention away from yourself was a nice touch. But getting back to the afternoon of the farmers' shoot: After Dinsdale took the drink, you left him alone for fifteen or twenty minutes to give the poison time to act, then you came back to check on him. The poor visibility that day was a fortuitous development but not essential to your plans. You knew, due to the nature of the terrain, that neither Dinsdale's shooting butt nor your own could be seen from the next butt over. It wasn't a pretty sight, was it, Mick? Mr. Dinsdale lying there on the grass, convulsing in his own vomit. That's when you went to phase two of the operation. You removed the loose stone from the wall of the butt where you'd previously imprisoned an adder. Then you took Dinsdale's right arm and thrust his hand into the cavity. The snake, predictably incensed at having its territory invaded, did its job. That's where it started to go wrong, isn't that right, Mick?"

"I don't know what you're talking about," Curtis said evenly.

"Either you were careless or the snake got away from you, but you ended up getting bitten, as well. On the right hand, I suspect. Katie Elger distinctly remembers you raising your left arm to point when she asked you what was wrong that afternoon, yet I've seen myself that you're right-handed."

Curtis sneered at him. "Tell me something, Mr. Sherlock bloody Holmes: Why would I want to murder my employer? It'd be a little like killing the goose that laid the golden egg, wouldn't it?"

Powell nodded. "That is a bit of a poser, all right. It struck me right from the start that you were the only person to have anything good to say about him. But then you didn't have any reason to complain, did you, Mick? He'd promoted you to head keeper—not because you deserved it, but to punish Harry Settle. And you'd even managed to insinuate yourself into his stepsister's bed. I'd say you had a good thing going."

The gamekeeper's eyes narrowed. "You know something? You're beginning to get on my frigging nerves."

"So why *would* you want to kill him?" Powell persisted. "It wasn't the water scheme, was it? You couldn't care less about the impact on the residents of Brackendale. In fact, you would benefit from the development. Recreational Director at the Blackamoor Hall Hotel in the scenic North York Moors National Park, offering traditional grouse shooting on the moors and a range of water sports on our newly created lake. Personal instruction can be arranged. I could write the brochure."

Curtis smiled, but his eyes were cold. "Not much of a motive for killing him, then, is it, Chief Superintendent?"

"I think it's true you and Dinsdale got along famously—you were two of a kind, in fact—each using the other to further your own interests. The one thing you didn't count on was Dinsdale's highly developed sense of class consciousness. It's ironic, isn't it, since he was new money himself, but to Dickie you were just another one of the hired help. When he found out you were having an affair with Felicity, even though there was no love lost between them, he viewed it as an affront, if not an actual threat to his position. He told Felicity he was going to sack you at the end of the shooting season when he no longer needed you. It's my guess that she told you about his plans."

Curtis, stone-faced, said nothing.

Powell shook his head. "All your prospects down the drain. You couldn't allow that to happen, could you, Mick? By getting rid of Dinsdale you'd kill two birds with one stone. Keeping your position and ensuring that Felicity eventually inherits the estate. If you'd played your cards right, you might well have ended up lord of the manor someday. You only made one mistake. When Katie surprised you after you'd killed the snake, you reacted by attempting to cover up the fact that you'd been bitten. It worked in your favor at first, creating the impression that you were so upset about Mr. Dinsdale that you got physically sick. In actual fact, you were displaying the classic symptoms of an adder bite."

Curtis laughed harshly. "It's an interesting theory, I'll give you that, but you don't have a shred of proof. None of it would stand up in court."

"Perhaps you can call Francesca Aguirre as a character witness," Powell commented.

Curtis shrewdly regarded Powell. "You do get around, Chief Superintendent."

Once again Powell's gaze took in the rolling expanse of moorland beyond the gamekeeper. "Why don't you just confess, Mick, and save the taxpayers a lot of bother?" he said. "If you show sufficient remorse, you could be out in fifteen years."

Curtis seemed to mull this over for a few moments. Then he sighed. "All right, you win. I'll come along quietly." He thrust his shovel into the mound of grit and then looked at Powell. "You have no idea what it's like for people like me, do you? I spent my bloody youth in Sheffield on the dole, without a hope in the world of finding decent work. As a boy I used to spend the summers working on my uncle's farm in Wensleydale, so I knew a bit about shooting. When I got the job of assistant underkeeper at Blackamoor, it was a chance for a fresh start, to work myself up and make something of myself."

Powell could think of nothing to say.

Curtis walked over to his Land Rover. "I'll give you a lift back to the shooting box." He reached for the door handle and opened it.

Before Powell could react, Curtis had picked up the shotgun that was lying across the seat and turned to face him. Powell stared into the twin black holes of the over-and-under's muzzle.

The gamekeeper smiled. "Say your frigging prayers, copper."

Powell drew a shallow breath. "Don't be foolish, Mick. Sergeant Evans knows I've come up here to see you. You're just making it worse for yourself," Powell said, with an air of bravado he did not feel.

"I know a little bog where you'll sink out of sight and never be seen again," Curtis said, his voice chillingly devoid of emotion.

"They'll find my car at the shooting box. They'll figure it out," Powell argued, trying to buy some time.

Curtis affected an expression of mock concern. "I was up there working, all right, but I didn't see Mr. Powell. He must have got there after I left and wandered off somewhere."

"No one will believe you."

"I've got nothing to lose, have I?"

Powell tensed his muscles. "It was a nice try, Mick, but here come my reinforcements now." He looked over the gamekeeper's shoulder.

Curtis sneered. "You don't think I'm going to fall for the oldest trick in the book—"

A voice suddenly rolled across the moor. "Hello, Erskine!"

Keeping the barrels pointed at Powell's chest, Curtis turned his head to look. A figure was emerging from a dip in the moor about fifty yards off and walking towards them. It was all Powell needed. He brought the gamekeeper down with a flying tackle. The shotgun discharged close to Powell's head with a deafening boom. He somehow managed to get on top, struggling fiercely to wrest the shotgun from his opponent's grasp. As they grappled in the heather, Curtis, with his superior strength, managed to twist the gun around from a port arms position so that it was now pointing between their faces. Slowly and inexorably, he forced the muzzle towards Powell's head. "Say good-bye, mate," he said between clenched teeth.

The next thing Powell heard was a gruff expletive, and then from out of nowhere a swinging boot caught Curtis on the side of the head with a solid thud. The gamekeeper's eyes fluttered and he went limp under Powell's body.

Heaving for air, Powell looked up into a grinning, bearded face. "Hello, Alex," he said with as much dignity as he could muster. "What brings you to the North York Moors?"

The Scot shook his head sadly. "The riffraff they allow on an English grouse moor these days."

With a painful grunt, Powell rolled off Curtis and pushed himself to his knees. He lifted the gamekeeper's right wrist and pulled off the tatty fingerless glove. There, on the back of his hand, partially healed but still visible, were two small puncture wounds.

EPILOGUE

As Barrett explained it, he had decided, more or less on the spur of the moment, to surprise Powell, whom he reckoned would be sorely in need of a wee break. After arranging a day of walked-up shooting on nearby Rosedale Moor, he'd piled into his aging Escort the day before and driven nonstop from Inverness to the North York Moors. He had rung Marion to find out where Powell was staying, and when he'd checked at the Lion and Hippo that morning, Robert Walker had fortuitously directed him to East Moor. In a celebratory mood in the Lion and Hippo that evening, Powell and Barrett even managed to convince a reluctant Sarah Evans to accompany them on their grouse shoot the following day.

It was a glorious autumn morning and the moor was spread out before them like a tapestry of russet and green; there wasn't a cloud in the sky and a tiny merlin,

the first Powell had ever seen, glided gracefully overhead, searching for meadow pipits. The only thing
missing was a certain Gordon setter named Misty.

"Over there—to the left!" Barrett shouted.

Powell saw a flash of black and tan as their so-called
hunting dog—rented to them for the day by the moor
owner—appeared for an instant, feathery black tail
waving excitedly above the heather, before disappearing
again over the horizon. "I'll see if I can catch up to her,"
he called out to Barrett and Sarah Evans as he struck out
for the spot where he'd last glimpsed their faithful companion. Walking over springy stems of heather between
scattered blocks of gray lichen-stained rock, he climbed
towards the crest of the moor.

As he picked his way up the slope, breathing heavily,
he couldn't help speculating about the ancestry of Spaun-
ton's Regal Mistress, or Misty for short. The Duke of
Gordon, the originator of the breed, was reputed to have
crossed one of his dogs with a bloodhound to increase
the scenting ability of his line. Judging by Misty's turbo-
charged performance, Powell suspected that the canny
old Scot had slipped in a bit of greyhound as well.

He eventually reached the top and a welcome breeze
cooled his perspiring face. He looked down at a gentle
slope of heather, which fell away more steeply near the
bottom into the rock-strewn course of a tumbling gill.
His eyes scanned the hillside, but there was no sign of the
dog. The vast silence was pierced by a curlew's wild cry.
He rested his gun on his shoulder and started down the
slope, whistling and calling to no avail. When he got to a
point just above the stream, he stopped to listen. There

was nothing but the sound of rushing water. He looked back up the hillside and saw Barrett and Sarah coming over the top.

Before starting back, he walked down to the edge of the stream to get a drink. Just as he was about to lay down his gun, he happened to glance upstream. There, about ten yards from where he stood and partially screened by a tangle of gorse, was Misty, frozen on point. She was as rigid as if she'd been sculpted from a block of marble, her brain hardwired to lock up at the first intoxicating scent of her quarry. Not taking his eyes off her, Powell slipped two cartridges into the breech of his gun and quietly closed the action. At the soft *click* of the gun being loaded, Misty began to tremble with anticipation, but her gaze remained fixed on a patch of heather about twenty feet in front of her nose on the far bank of the stream.

Powell made his way carefully over to the dog, searching the cover for any hint of where the objects of her attention might lie. He was trying to decide where to cross over the gill when there was a sudden flurry of wings as a covey of grouse exploded from the heather. *Brr-beck-a-beck, beck, beck, beck, go-back, go-back.*

He pushed off the safety catch as the old Westley Richards came up to his shoulder and swung the barrels out in front of the lead bird. He could see the chestnut and black of the grouse's breast and the vermilion over its eye as clearly as if he were looking at a painting. He watched the covey disappear from view then slowly lowered his gun. He broke open the action and extracted the cartridges. Enough to be alive amidst this wild splendor, he thought.

He looked down into Misty's recriminating brown eyes and wondered how he was going to explain himself to Barrett.

A CONVERSATION WITH
GRAHAM THOMAS

Q: Graham, who (or what) was the inspiration for your series hero, Detective-Chief Superintendent Erskine Powell of New Scotland Yard?

A: Powell is undoubtedly an amalgam of various influences and experiences, both literary and personal. It became apparent when I started writing *Malice in the Highlands*, the first book in the series, that he already existed somewhere in my creative unconscious. It's as if I'm writing about someone I know intimately, as opposed to consciously constructing a fictional character.

Q: Let's talk briefly about your pre-Powell life. Would you give us a thumbnail biography of yourself?

A: From the moment I picked up a copy of J. P. Donleavy's *The Ginger Man* as an impressionable youth, I knew I wanted to be a writer. I majored in English literature at university, then switched to biology when I realized that I might have to get a job someday. For the past twenty-five years, I've worked as a professional biologist in the field of fisheries management.

Q: When you introduced Erskine Powell in Malice in the Highlands, *did you envision a series? Or was* Highlands *originally a stand-alone novel?*

A: I always envisioned a series. There are the practical considerations, of course, but from a creative point of view, much of the enjoyment I derive from writing mysteries is the opportunity to continually develop and reveal my hero's character, to test him in new situations. You can't do this in a one-off novel. Also, I think most mystery readers appreciate continuity. It's like cheering on the home team—although every game is different, the star player never lets you down.

Q: Clearly you are not (and never have been, have you?) a Scotland Yard detective; but that aside, how much of Erskine Powell is based on your own experience? Or to ask another way: In what ways is your protagonist similar to—and completely unlike—his creator?

A: Short of signing up for a course of psychoanalysis, I'm not sure how I should answer that! Powell is better-educated, better-looking, and more intuitive than I am. However, like his creator, he is, beneath a somewhat cynical veneer, a romantic at heart. More revealing, perhaps, is the fact that we're both addicted to curry.

Q: What about background research—how vital is that for you?

A: Getting the details right is very important to me. Put it down to my scientific training. Having said that, I am willing to sacrifice verisimilitude, where necessary, to further the story. An example: In my books, Powell is a member of the Yard's Murder Squad, an organization which no longer exists. At one time, senior Scotland Yard detectives called in by local police forces to investigate difficult or high-profile murder cases, but this is no longer the case. It is, nonetheless, a useful fictional device which enables me to set my stories in a variety of interesting and atmospheric locales such as the Scottish Highlands, the north coast of Cornwall, and the North York Moors. I typically spend more time doing background research for a book and thinking about the story in a fairly unstructured way than actually writing.

Q: Your novels unfold in actual locales, although you sometimes invent town names. What advantages and disadvantages have you discovered with this approach?
A: A vivid sense of place and setting is (I hope) a key element of my novels. In order to strike a balance between realism and literary license, I generally set my stories in a fictional village, which I locate—using plausible, but not overly precise, geographic reference points—near a real town. For example, *Malice in Cornwall* features the imaginary village of Penrick near St. Ives. Similarly, *Malice on the Moors* is set in and around the fictional hamlet of Brackendale, near the town of Kirkbymoorside in North Yorkshire. This approach enables me to realistically describe an actual locale yet allows me to take liberties for plot purposes. And I don't have to worry about somebody who was born and raised in my village taking me to task for getting some detail wrong. The disadvantage? The risk of not pulling if off.

Q: You chose a pseudonym for your novels. What was the thinking behind that?
A: Being a writer with a day job, I basically have a split personality. A pseudonym seemed the logical expression of this. And it has the added advantage of insulating one from excessive public adulation or derision. (I like to hedge my bets!)

Q: What's the game plan for you—and Erskine Powell—after **Malice on the Moors?**
A: Erskine and I have a number of ideas, including a story set in London and perhaps a trip to America.

*If you enjoyed
this Erskine Powell mystery,*

*don't miss
his earlier adventures!*

MALICE
IN THE HIGHLANDS

On holiday from his job as Detective-Chief Superintendent of New Scotland Yard, Erskine Powell embarks on a salmon-fishing competition in the Scottish Highlands.

But there, in the castle-dotted countryside along the picturesque River Spey, a cold-blooded murder soon turns Powell's haven into a busman's holiday—and a quiet anglers' paradise becomes just as deadly as the mean streets of London.

MALICE IN THE HIGHLANDS
by
GRAHAM THOMAS

Published by The Ballantine Publishing Group.
Available at your local bookstore.